MOON SONG

An Evans Novel of Romance

MOON SONG

SONJA MASSIE

M. EVANS & COMPANY, INC. NEW YORK

Library of Congress Cataloging-in-Publication Data

Massie, Sonja.

Moon Song / Sonja Massie.
p.   cm.—(An Evans novel of romance)
ISBN 0-87131-608-0   : $15.95
I. Title.   II. Series.
PS3563.A7998M66   1990   90-37049
813'.54—dc20   CIP

M. Evans and Company, Inc.
216 East 49 Street
New York, New York 10017

Manufactured in the United States of America

2 4 6 8 9 7 5 3 1

Lovingly dedicated
to
GWENDOLYNN and BILL,

Who are young enough at heart
And old enough in spirit
To believe in magic

The author would like to thank WILLIAM ARMSTRONG, an authority on medieval history, whose contributions added so much to this novel.

And thank you to ARDEN MASSIE for the oven-warm chocolate-chip cookies and the occasional hug that raised my spirits . . . and my blood sugar level.

One

THE YOUNG WOMAN crept silently among the dark trees, her body tense, her ears straining for any unusual sounds in the forest. If anyone saw her gathering herbs by the light of a full moon, she would lose her life. According to the laws of Hamelin, she was committing the sin of heresy, of blasphemy . . . of witchcraft.

Silver rays streamed through the breaks in the branches over her head, bathing her in a mystic blue light. As she walked, the hem of her skirt swirled the fog that lay in patches on the mossy ground. She pushed back a strand of the black hair that cascaded in waves down her shoulders, to her waist. Just above her right temple a white streak of hair glistened among the black, the sign of the devil—or so said the villagers.

The woman worked slowly, selecting her herbs with care, a scowl of concentration crossing her pretty face. She smiled as she placed a sprig of wolfsbane, some gort leaves, and holly berries into her basket beside the night's most valuable find, the elusive man root.

For a moment the moon slid behind the clouds, and the girl shivered as she sensed a disturbing ripple in the tranquillity of the forest, an uneasiness that trickled cold across her skin. She peered over her right shoulder, then her left, searching the darkness for the evil that had invaded her wooded sanctuary.

She smelled it first—the putrid stench of sulfuric gases that choked her and caused her to drop her basket. Clutching her throat, she fell to her knees as the moonlit woods faded from her sight and a vision of thick, suffocating darkness engulfed her.

Voices echoed through her head, the frightened whispers of children trapped in a black labyrinth. The murmurings quickly crescendoed into screams of fear and pain, mixed with the roar of a mountain as it collapsed. The young woman gasped as terror gripped her, squeezed her. Their pain became hers as stone and dirt rained about them, crushing the life from their frail bodies, and poisonous gases robbed them of breath.

It had happened; the realization swept over her as she knelt there on the damp moss and sobbed.

The witch's prophecy had been fulfilled, after all.

In the stark brilliance of the morning sun the tragedy was even worse than Leisel Kistner had expected. On the outskirts of the village of Hamelin at the base of Koppelberg Mountain lay more wounded and dying children than she could allow her heart to count. Pauper children. Miners—most of them too young to have passed even a decade on earth.

One of the main tunnels had collapsed during the night, and the survivors, the brothers and sisters of the victims, were still dragging bodies from the bowels of the mountain.

Leisel and the other adults could only watch. The narrow passages wouldn't accommodate their bodies, as the tunnels had been dug by children, for children. Small bodies required less room, less digging, and children cost the mine owner less to house and feed than adults. Besides, in Lower

Saxony in 1274, a pauper child was an inexpensive commodity, often bought with the price of a loaf of bread. In a world plagued by poverty, few commoners could afford the burden of another hungry mouth. The needy sold their children to the wealthy mine owners, thinking their sons and daughters would at least have food and clothing, luxuries that impoverished fathers were unable to provide. Parents were blissfully unaware of the horrors of daily life in the mines, and they tried not to think about cave-ins.

Leisel watched in stunned horror as, one by one, the children were pulled from the dark tunnel. She knew and loved many of these children, and her heart wept for each limp body that was laid upon the grassy knoll at the foot of the mountain. So much suffering. So many dead, and for no reason. This shouldn't have happened; her mother had warned the citizens of Hamelin, but they had hardened their hearts—and killed the prophet.

"No . . . God in heaven, no," she whispered as she moved along the rows, recognizing face after grime-blackened face among the victims. Her fear increasing by the moment, she searched for one child in particular, one set of bright blue eyes, one small heart-shaped face among so many.

"Have you found her yet?" A gentle hand was laid on Leisel's arm, and she turned to see her own grief reflected in another's eyes.

"No, Helga, I haven't found her." Leisel fought the urge to fall into the old woman's arms and sob. This was no time for grief; there were children to comfort, wounds to bandage, and bones to set. In spite of her sorrow, Leisel was relieved to see Helga's wizened face. The old woman was strange—even moon-crazed, the villagers claimed—but she had taught Leisel and her mother before her about the magic of the herbs of the forest and the flowers of the fields. Leisel welcomed her presence and her knowledge of healing in the midst of this calamity.

"Your little Monika is alive," Helga said, patting Leisel's arm.

"Have you seen her?" Leisel didn't dare to hope that the child who had been like a younger sister to her could be living and whole.

"I saw her . . . in here." She tapped her forehead with one gnarled forefinger. "She's alive, I tell you."

Leisel relaxed a bit, knowing what the old woman meant. Helga often saw things that no one else could see. Sometimes Leisel experienced these visions, too, though she tried not to. People who saw too much sometimes lost their lives in Hamelin—as Leisel knew all too well.

Slipping several small pouches of herbs and powders into Leisel's apron, along with a roll of linen strips, Helga whispered, "Come along now, there's work to be done. Just don't let the good Father Beck catch you."

Leisel nodded and tried unsuccessfully to put thoughts of Monika aside as she moved from child to child, offering what solace she could in the form of a bandage, a poultice, a mug of water, a comforting word.

"Ah, little Hans," she said as she gingerly palpated a boy's swollen, bruised leg. "Your eyes are bright with pain."

"It hurts dreadful bad," the child replied in a high-pitched voice stretched thin from infrequent use. Many of the children who worked the mine had high, squeaky voices. Speaking wasn't allowed in the tunnels. Communication interfered with the all-important work at hand, that of bringing gold out of Koppelberg Mountain.

"It seems you were one of the lucky ones," she said as she bathed his dirty, gnomelike face with her kerchief, which she'd dipped in the river that flowed nearby. "At least you're alive and your limbs aren't broken."

"Where's my brother?" the boy asked, lifting his head and glancing across the scores of prone bodies. "Have you seen my brother Sigmund?"

"No, I haven't, *liebchen*. Have you seen Monika?"

He nodded and winced from the pain the movement caused. "I passed her in the tunnel when I was crawling out. She was crying. Said her arm was hurt."

"But she was alive?"

"She was then. But after that another part of the tunnel came down, so I don't know what became of her."

Leisel could see that every word was an agony for the boy, so she pressed him back to the ground with a gentle hand on his bony chest. Smoothing the tousled blond hair back from his forehead, she said, "Just lie still and try not to worry. I'll ask the other children if anyone has seen him."

For hours Leisel, Helga, and several other women from the village nursed the injured children as still more corpses were pulled from the mountain. The cries of the injured echoed down the hill and across the green meadows, along with the creaking of the wagon wheels as load after load of stones and debris was cleared away.

Periodically pungent gasses and clouds of dust billowed from the mine shaft, and Leisel shuddered, thinking of Monika, still trapped in that hell. "Live, little one," she whispered, trying to send a bit of her own strength into that dark tunnel. "I'm waiting for you out here in the sunshine. Don't give up."

The hours passed and the summer sun beat down on Leisel's head, but she continued to work . . . and hope . . . and pray.

"I tried to save my sister," one girl sobbed as Leisel held her head so that she could sip water from a ladle. "But the rocks were falling all around us and it was so dark that I couldn't see her. She was holding on to my hand, but she let go."

"Don't cry, little one," Leisel said, rocking the girl in her arms. "You tried to help her but you couldn't. It wasn't your fault."

"We all know whose fault it was," said one of the older boys who had escaped serious injury and was helping Leisel by hauling water from the river. "It was Baron Schmidt's fault. He knew the mine wasn't safe, but he forced us to work down there in that black, stinking hell. God damn his eyes, I say."

"It's a grave sin to curse your benefactor," said a stringy, nasal voice behind Leisel. She rose, and her stomach knotted when she saw Father Beck standing behind her, his long thin arms folded across the front of his cowl-necked tunic. His dark eyes swept over her, one bushy eyebrow cocked suspiciously. "What are you doing to those children?"

He nodded toward the wad of bandages in Leisel's hand, and she clasped the linen strips to her chest. He couldn't see inside the pockets of her apron, she reminded herself. Although he claimed to be the right hand of God ruling over mere mortals, Leisel sensed his limitations and knew he couldn't see the herbs and poultices she had secreted there.

"The wrath of heaven and earth will be upon your head if you use any of the devil's devices, like spells or potions, on these young ones." He absently scratched at a festering rash on his spindly forearm.

To avoid looking at the unsightly red rash, Leisel stared into his rheumy eyes. She knew that a poultice of duir leaves and quert pulp would take away the itch and heal his affliction. However, she knew that if she offered him the remedy, her life would be in jeopardy for practicing witchcraft. Other women in the village of Hamelin had died for less.

"I only want to help these children, not harm them," she said, wishing she could simply walk away from him. But no one turned their back on Father Beck. As emissary of God and the Church, the priest wielded more power than any member of the town council, even Hamelin's mayor, Baron Schmidt.

The priest scratched again at the rash, his long yellowed

fingernails drawing a few drops of blood. "There are those of us who believe that you are responsible for this calamity."

Leisel had expected the accusation. She certainly wasn't the first young woman in Hamelin to be blamed when a tragedy had befallen the town. But anticipation hadn't prepared her for the wash of fear that left her legs weak as she listened to the priest's words of condemnation.

"How could you even think I would bring such suffering to so many innocent children?" Her eyes scanned the rows of tiny, broken bodies, then looked down at the child she had just ministered to, who lay at her feet. "Would I be out here now, nursing the wounded, if I had somehow brought on this catastrophe?"

He sniffed and rubbed his bulbous nose, reddened from years of sampling the communion wine. "You'd do anything to avenge your mother's death," he said. The coldness in his tone chilled her. It was like a voice from the grave—her grave, if she wasn't careful.

Reaching into the sleeve of his robe, he extracted an engraved silver flask that contained holy water. With great ceremony he sprinkled some on himself and then on her shoulders, watching her closely all the while. What did he expect? she wondered. Did he suppose that when the water touched her she would shriek blasphemies like one possessed of a demon? Did he expect the blessed anointment would scald her evil flesh?

She stood for a long moment, staring into those inscrutable dark eyes. "My mother is dead," she said quietly and without inflection. "Nothing can restore her to life. And no goodness can be wrought by the deaths of these children."

From the corner of her eye she saw the cooper's wife and the tavern mistress watching and listening. Why was she always the center of this town's attention? First it had been her mother, now her. Had the villagers nothing better to do than scrutinize her with those hungry eyes that made her feel as though she were about to be devoured?

As the priest turned to administer last rites to the dead and dying children, Leisel wondered, as she had many times these past six years, what she had done to deserve this village's hatred.

What had her mother done to deserve death?

Leisel looked down at the children lying at her feet and up toward the mine entrance, where Helga was helping with the wounded that were being loaded onto wagons, and she realized that she wasn't completely alone and unloved in this village. Her enemies were many, but so were her friends. As long as even one of these children needed her help, she had a reason for living.

"Leisel!" shouted Hans, the boy whose leg she had bound. He was gesturing wildly to her from his resting place on the thick green grass. "Leisel, look! It's Monika!"

Whirling around to see where he was pointing, Leisel saw a welcome sight that caused her eyes to flood with tears of relief and thanksgiving. She dropped the bundle of bandages and the water ladle and flew up the hill, her skirts billowing around her.

Old Helga stood beside a pile of boulders at the mine entrance, her arm supporting a girl with thick auburn curls and amber eyes that were round with pain and fear.

"Monika!" Leisel cried as she folded the girl to her chest and held her close. "Let me look at you. Are you hurt, *liebchen*?"

The child's faint smile shone through the thick layer of dirt and grime that darkened her tiny face. "My arm hurts, but I made it out alive."

Leisel and Helga examined the injured arm and saw a deep gash, but the bone was intact and Monika appeared to have no other injuries.

"That's a fearsome cut," Helga told Leisel. "You'll have to keep a close watch on it."

"I will," Leisel said as she examined the girl's wound. "You've made it this far, little one, and I'll see to it that your arm is whole again."

"It was terrible." The girl buried her face against Leisel's bodice and began to cry, her small, frail body racked with sobs. "It was so dark, and the other children were screaming, and the rocks were falling. I had to climb over some of them to get out . . . and I think they were dead."

"It's all right. It's over now and you're safe."

The girl lifted her head and looked up at Leisel, her tears making black, muddy tracks down her cheeks. "I heard you calling me, Leisel," she said. "I heard you telling me not to give up. I heard you telling me to keep crawling until I saw the sunshine."

Leisel dropped to her knees and held the child tightly to her, as though afraid she would be snatched away. For the first time that day she allowed her own tears to fall. She wept for the children who had been lost or maimed. But she also cried tears of joy for those who had been spared, like the child she held in her arms, her sister in ways that were more binding than blood ties.

This child needed her. Looking around at the little ones who had been wounded in body, mind, and spirit, Leisel realized that they all needed her. Let Father Beck and the rest of the town stand against her; she wouldn't back down. She would stay here in this village and fight for these children. A catastrophe like this must never happen again.

She could feel his eyes on her as she moved around the table serving the savory pork-and-garlic stew. Of all the eyes in the village, Baron Werner Schmidt's were the hungriest. Leisel cringed every time they raked over her, from her bodice to her feet and back.

"You're to appear before the town council for examination one week from today, Leisel," he said as he picked up a ham hock and gnawed on it like one of the feral dogs who tore at the raw scraps thrown to them from the window of the meat shop. He tossed the bone onto the table, picked another hock from the bowl, and wiped the grease from his dewlaps with the sleeve of his tunic. "The talk in the town is that you caused my mine to collapse."

"Leisel couldn't have caused such a thing," said Schmidt's daughter from her seat at his left hand. Trudl's lashless brown eyes widened with fear, but her indignation was as evident in her voice as her loyalty to Leisel.

"You'll keep mum!" Schmidt lifted a beefy fist, and Trudl ducked her head in a defensive, practiced gesture.

At the other end of the table the baron's wife cleared her throat delicately. Everything about Eva Schmidt was delicate: her heart-shaped face, her doelike eyes, her dainty figure. She was a fragile gentlewoman—or so said the kindest souls in Hamelin. The others simply called her weak.

"Leisel *wouldn't* have done such a thing, even if she were able," she added in a timid half whisper that only Leisel could hear.

"Well, you'd better not have caused it," Herr Schmidt said, turning his head to glimpse down Leisel's bodice as she leaned across him to sprinkle salt shavings on his meat. "Every day that mine is closed, I lose a pretty bag of coins. It'll be weeks before those little sluggards will have the tunnel cleared again."

Leisel felt her stomach twist into a knot around the waxen bit of cheese she had eaten for dinner, a servant's meal, so different from the elaborate spread of soup, breads, cheeses, and fruits she had prepared for the Schmidts. "You're not going to reopen the mine, are you?" she asked.

"Really, Werner," Eva said, raising her soft voice imperceptibly, "you can't be serious. So many of the children were killed today. We can't risk it happening again."

"Tunnel collapse is to be expected from time to time."

Schmidt sniffed and rubbed his crooked nose with the back of his hand. "The occasional cave-in and loss of workers is simply part of mining."

Her hand trembling with anger and fatigue, Leisel set the bowl of salt on the table. She couldn't forget those gaunt faces, the small, mangled bodies of her friends. The haunting image made her bolder than usual. "Those children died today because the mine—*your mine*—wasn't safe. Doesn't that matter at all to you?"

Eva and Trudl gasped, and the room fell silent. Schmidt sat quietly for a moment, as though unable to speak. Then he brought his fist down on the table with a thud that sent the wooden bowls bouncing and overturned Trudl's pewter wine cup. "Need I remind you, girl, that you are a servant in my household? I'll not have my judgment or my morals questioned by a scullery maid, the daughter of the devil's whore."

Trudl shot a startled look down the table at Eva, whose pinched face turned a shade paler.

Leisel said nothing but stood, hands clenched into fists beneath her apron, staring at the man who dared to call her evil when he had brought more suffering into the world than anyone she had known. Swallowing the bitter words that rose in her throat, she turned and walked into the kitchen, slamming the door behind her. As she entered, half a dozen rats scurried for cover behind the ale kegs and the bread board.

Rats . . . they seemed to be everywhere these days. Where were the cats that had always kept them under control? Leisel shivered as she remembered. The cats had met the same end as their owners—those beautiful young women with strange healing powers in their hands, women who knew the magic of the forest's herbs, women who murmured incantations beneath the light of a full moon. Many of these women had used their esoteric knowledge for the good of others . . . and had died for the privilege.

Leisel tried not to think about those women as she sat on a three-legged stool beside the fireplace. There were too many similarities between herself and them. If she weren't careful, she would meet the same end.

Leisel held her hands out to the flames that licked the bottom of the soup pot that simmered there day and night. But after holding her hands there only a moment, she snatched them back and buried them in her apron. Tears flooded her eyes as she remembered her mother's slanted green eyes, which had always glittered with the simple joy of living; her beautiful black hair, which had turned silver almost overnight.

Fire would always remind Leisel of her mother . . . and of how she had died. Every time she looked into those dancing flames, she would remember what the citizens of Hamelin had done to her.

Her mother, Katrina Kistner, had been one of those young women with healing in her hands. Her mother. Accused of being the devil's whore.

That made Leisel the devil's bastard daughter. At least everyone she knew thought so.

And for all Leisel knew, they were right.

For six days Leisel nursed the wounded miner children while trying not to neglect her duties to the Schmidt household. As each dawn broke, she was in the makeshift shed that had been thrown together for their convalescence, changing bandages and poultices and drying their tears. An hour later she was back at the baron's estate, washing laundry, preparing meals, and scrubbing the house, which was the largest in the village.

At the end of her exhausting day Leisel attempted to sleep, desperately trying not to think about the coming examination before the town council. But her mind kept running ahead to the future, anticipating their accusations, rehearsing her defense.

Other times her thoughts returned to the past and the painful memories stored there. Although the council had given her mother a death sentence, Leisel's life had been spared. Now that she could no longer hide behind the cloak of innocent youth, could she expect to find the same charity in the hearts of her fellow villagers?

She remembered her mother, standing tall, proud, and elegant before the council with her eleven-year-old daughter at her side. Leisel would never forget the moment when Baron Schmidt and Father Beck had uttered the one word that had condemned her mother to death. They had spoken many words that morning, but "witch" was the only one that the young Leisel had understood, the only word she remembered after all this time. Six years later the memory of that night still caused a sick, hollow feeling deep in her chest.

They couldn't convict her without some proof of her guilt, could they? She asked herself the question over and over as she lay on her pallet of straw, looking up through the mullioned window at the moon that hung low in the sky.

Somehow the moon's mystic, feminine presence comforted her, soothed her troubled spirit. She remembered something that her mother had told her once about "dancing with the moon." Katrina Kistner had said that the moon sent her own song to the earth on glistening beams, a song that sparkled like silver and answered the deepest needs of a woman's heart.

Leisel hadn't understood her mother's words then, and even now, as she lay on her pallet and looked up at the glowing orb, the true meaning eluded her. She lifted her right hand and held her palm up to the sky, trying to absorb the light and power of those silver beams.

"Help me," she whispered, bathed in the comfort of a maternal presence that she hadn't felt for such a long time—

not since her mother had last held her in her arms. "Please
. . . help me."

As she raced through the dark trees she clutched the
leather-bound journal to her chest and fought for breath.
She had been running for a long time, and her sides ached
terribly. Sweat streamed down her face, stinging her eyes and
temporarily blinding her. The wind whipped her rain-
sodden skirt around her legs as she stumbled through the
woods, tripping over the thick ferns and gnarled tree roots.

Deep in the back of her mind, a voice told her that she
was dreaming. But the danger was no less terrifying. If they
caught her, she would die. In the distance she could hear the
angry roar of the mob, a blood-hungry pack that had been
denied the satisfaction of the kill. At least for the moment.

Ignoring the pain that stabbed at her ribs, she took a deep
breath and raced out of the forest and across a moonlit pas-
ture. She had reached the edge of the meadow when she
heard it . . . the moon's song. It was silver, as her mother had
said, a melody that she recognized deep in her spirit. She
knew every shimmering note as it drifted toward her on the
night wind and lured her into the forest. To the trees. To
safety. To him.

The moon had heard her, after all, and sent help.

Two

FAR AWAY, IN a castle set deep in the Bohemian Forest, a man awoke from a horrifying dream. He bolted upright in his bed as his fists clenched the sweat-soaked linens. His spirit churning, he yanked the heavy bed draperies aside and walked naked across the bedchamber to the window.

His golden hair and muscular body glistened in the moonlight as his pale blue eyes scanned the countryside. Beneath his castle wall, vineyards heavy with unharvested fruit scented the night air with the rich smell of wine. And beyond the vineyards, foothills stretched to the jagged black mountains that marked the edge of his domain.

A movement just beneath the castle gate caught his eye, and he watched in fascination as a giant silver wolf paced the length of the wall. For a moment the animal paused and looked up at the window where the man stood. Then it lifted its muzzle and howled, a sound that chilled the warm summer-night air.

As though coming to a decision, the man abruptly turned from the window, walked across the room, and removed some garments from an ornately carved chest in the corner. With the agility of a hunter he slipped on heavy wool hose and a linen shirt. Reaching into the chest once more, he removed a leather pouch heavy with coins, a silver goblet, a slender oak rod, and a short sword. Placing these items atop the clothing on the bed, he gathered the bundle together and tied it with a rope.

As he worked, the man's face registered his anger and determination—the emotional residue left by his dream. He had heard the screams of the innocents and vowed it would never happen again. On a table in the corner of the room he found a golden box with a jeweled crest emblazoned across its lid, a shield with a stag's head in the center. He raised the top, reached inside the box, and pulled out a sparkling length of silver—a flute.

For a moment his long slender fingers glided over the delicate instrument. From the box he lifted a sash of crimson silk, looped the scarf through a notch on the pipe, then draped the sash around his neck.

Across the foot of the bed lay a cloak, its myriad bright colors glowing, muted pastels in the moonlight. Without hesitation the man lifted the cloak and threw it around his broad shoulders.

Then, tucking the bundle under his arm, he made his way silently through the dark corridors of the castle. None of the servants—not even the guards at the heavy, fortified door—inquired about his mission. The fire in his blue eyes and the set of his jaw stifled their curiosity.

Without a backward glance he strode across the drawbridge and into the vineyard, where he joined the silver wolf. Turning their faces to the moon, they headed toward the northwest.

Three

"KNOWING THAT GOD has the power to strike you dead where you stand if you lie, you must tell me now . . . did you bring about the collapse of Herr Schmidt's mine by use of the devil's magic?"

Inside her apron Leisel's hands knotted into fists, but her green eyes never wavered as she faced her accusers across the oak table. "I did not, Father Beck. I swear it on all that is holy."

The priest sniffed, lifted his vein-etched nose, and glanced down the table at the other members of the Hamelin town council. "And what could we expect the daughter of the devil to know about holy matters?"

Seated at the priest's left, Klaus Niklaus, the miller, stared down at his hands, which were white with oat flour. Goddard Wilheim, the town crier, was uncharacteristically quiet, without a word to say in Leisel's defense. The other members of the noble council merely shifted their feet, cleared their throats, and refused to meet her eye. If any member disagreed with Father Beck, none was willing to state his opinion or even allow it to show on his face. Everyone in the village acknowledged that the priest spoke the will and mind of God himself; he was not to be contradicted.

As she studied each of their faces in turn, Leisel wondered

if she had a friend among them. Once Rolf Gunter, the cooper, looked up at her and she thought she saw a shadow of compassion in his gray eyes, but he cast a sideways glance at Baron Schmidt and thereafter stared only at the solemn, forbidding row of hands that lay folded atop the trestle table.

The baron crossed his arms over his rotund belly, a mirthless smile creasing his face. "This council believes it was you who caused the catastrophe, Leisel," he said. "Your actions are unforgivable. I can't understand why you chose to repay my kindnesses to you with such evil."

Leisel thought of the six years of toil, cooking, scrubbing, and sewing for the Schmidt family. Six years of slavery seemed more than enough to pay for the meager evening portion of cheese or soup she received and the straw pallet in the stable. Not that she minded living the mean existence of a servant girl; she had been born to this life and she accepted her lot. It was the perverse attentions of her master that caused her such consternation. Gratitude wasn't an emotion easily summoned when she thought of Baron Schmidt's "kindnesses" to her.

She clenched her fists tighter, trying to hide her trembling. "If this council truly believed that I was guilty of witchcraft, I'd be dead this moment," she said. Her voice echoed through the council room, bringing a heavy silence in its wake. "Everyone in this village knows that the council requires no proof to convict the innocent. We knew that the day my mother was condemned to death."

The council members cringed and shifted miserably on their bench. Gunter glanced up at Leisel again, then toward the priest, who stared straight ahead, his rheumy eyes brimming with contempt and anger. Baron Schmidt still wore his bitter smile.

The silence grew heavier, interrupted only by the scuffling and squeaking of rats as they scrambled across the roof and played in the dark corners of the meeting room. But for once neither the council members nor Leisel noticed the rodents. The memory of a night six years before filled their minds, the image of a beautiful young woman with prematurely silver hair. A young woman whose left hand had been severed at the wrist. A woman who had pleaded not for her own life but for the life of her child.

Finally Schmidt spoke. "Your mother consorted with the devil, Leisel. You, of all people, know that. She cast spells on the good people of Hamelin, causing their cows to go dry, their crops to fail, and the men of this village to lose their potency. She never would have been able to visit such evil on this village had she not been a servant and mistress to the devil himself."

For a moment Leisel forgot that it was she who was being examined, that her life hung in the balance, offset only by the goodwill of the men seated before her. "That isn't true. My mother was a healer, a midwife whose hands brought children into this world and—"

"Enough of this," Father Beck roared, his gaunt face blushing scarlet. "That woman was proven to be evil. We found the marks on her body where she had actually suckled the devil. By the light of a full moon she was seen flying through the air on a pole dipped in the blood of a newborn babe. Using the devil's power, she changed her form into that of a wolf and attacked the baron himself. What more evidence did this honorable council need to convict her? But these matters have no importance in this proceeding. We're here to discuss *your* guilt or innocence. Not your mother's."

Cold reason washed over Leisel, and she softened her tone. "I *am* innocent. I swear, I know nothing of the evil you accuse me of committing."

The priest leaned across the table. His dark eyes speared her, but she refused to look away. "You know nothing of your mother's book?"

The book. Her heart lurched, but she fought to keep her

face expressionless. "I've told you before, Father, many times, I know nothing of any book."

"I want that book!" he shouted. The light of insanity flared in his eyes, sending fear burrowing deeper into Leisel's chest. "You have it. And someday you will give it to me."

"I've never seen such a book," she said with only the slightest tremor in her voice. "But if I had, why would you want to possess such a wicked thing?" Leisel didn't have to ask; she knew. There was power between those leather bindings, a power that Father Beck recognized and coveted.

He pressed his pale lips together in a thin line, as though fighting for control of his own demons. "I don't wish to possess it," he said tightly, "only to destroy it. And by the God above, I will."

He would destroy her, too. Leisel sensed his power and agitation as she faced him across the table. This man would never leave her in peace. This council and the people of Hamelin would keep watching her with their predatory eyes, waiting for the right moment to pounce, lusting for the chance to tear her to pieces.

As she stood before the council Leisel realized that she would eventually lose this war, that the day would come when this town would demand her life. But she would never surrender. They could kill her body but they couldn't destroy her spirit. So she spoke her mind, holding nothing back. "How much killing will it take to satisfy this council, this village? You've slain all the cats, believing them to be witches' familiars, and now our town is overrun by rats. You've killed every woman who tried to heal your sick with her knowledge of herbs and potions, and now your newborns die, and the mothers, too, and you wonder why. You killed my mother because she foretold a tragedy that could have been avoided but wasn't, and now there are fifty new graves on the hillside. More innocents dying. When will the killing stop?"

Slowly the priest rose, walked around the table, and stood beside her. He looked down at her with eyes that burned with a strange fire—all-consuming but without warmth. "There's at least one more who will die," he said. "We need only a little more evidence against you, Leisel Kistner. Make no mistake. It's this council's holy mission to search out the evil among us and destroy it. You won't escape divine justice in the end."

Leisel flinched inwardly to hear the words spoken aloud, but she didn't waver as she returned the priest's unblinking stare. Then, having made her quiet show of defiance, she turned her back on the noble councilmen of Hamelin and walked to the door. But before entering the dark hallway, she turned and said over her shoulder, "When you have your evidence, you know where to find me. All I ask is that you come for me in the light of day and that you execute me under the noonday sun, not in secret and in the darkest hour of the night . . . the way you murdered my mother." Her words echoed through the room as she whirled on her heel, exited the council chamber, and left the startled nobles staring dumbfounded after her.

In the hallway outside the chamber a man stood in the shadows. He was a stranger to Hamelin. Caught up in her own drama, Leisel didn't see him as she swept by, but he watched her intently, his pale blue eyes calculating the proud set of her chin; the firmness of her stride; her trembling hands, which were clenched at her side.

He smiled, pleased with the display of courage that he had just witnessed, and his fingers touched the silver length of pipe that hung around his neck.

As she left the building he hesitated only a moment, then stepped out of the shadows and followed her into the street.

Lost in her thoughts and fears, Leisel walked slowly through the village, unaware that she was being followed. If only she hadn't been so outspoken with the council. Those hasty words, uttered in blind anger, might cost her her life. If only they hadn't attacked her mother, she might have been able to control her temper, to stand there with downcast eyes and bowed head, to show them the picture of a defeated spirit, the only image they wanted to see. But they had said that her mother was evil—a false accusation that stung Leisel deeply. Throughout her childhood Leisel had witnessed an abundance of charitable deeds that her mother had done in her short life.

As Leisel walked the wheel-rutted, muddy street of Hamelin, past the livery, the church, and the inn, she saw more than a dozen villagers who owed their lives to her mother's healing. Playing in the streets were children whom her mother's skillful hands had brought into the world. Where were those children's grateful mothers the night her mother died?

Leisel remembered that some of them had been there, watching . . . with hungry eyes.

She shuddered and tried not to remember.

As she passed the crossroads in the center of the town she saw half a dozen women at the public well, drawing water. It had been a dry summer and the well was low. Leisel supposed she would be blamed for that, as well. She stared straight ahead as she walked by them, trying not to notice the suspicious glances, the anxious genuflecting, the whispers.

"Witch . . . white streak in her hair."

"Devil's daughter . . . caused the mine to cave in."

"Evil eye . . . don't look at her."

As quickly as she could, Leisel hurried past them, toward the southern wall of the village. After passing through the gate she crossed the bridge that spanned the River Weser and headed over the meadow toward the woods.

The village of Hamelin had never really been her home, she told herself. The townspeople would never allow her inside their community. She was different. Her mother had been different. And one paid a high price for the burden of being different in the village of Hamelin.

Leisel's spirit breathed a sigh of relief when she reached a stand of trees and was enveloped in the soothing, green silence of the forest. This was her home; she felt safe here, away from the examinations and accusations. Away from the whispered threats . . . and the hungry eyes.

He had followed her through the town, watching, wondering. His pale blue eyes missed nothing—the dour women at the well; the suspicious mothers that had shielded their children behind their skirts when she had walked by; the grizzled men who had gazed at her with open lust as she passed, then crossed themselves as though to ward off some unspeakable evil.

He watched as the young woman met the villagers' hostility with the same courage she had shown before the town council. Her back hadn't bent under the pressure, nor had her head bowed.

She wasn't merely beautiful; she was strong. She'll need to be strong, he thought grimly as he followed her through the village and over the bridge.

He wasn't surprised that she seemed to relax the moment she was surrounded by the trees of the forest. He knew this woman, had always known her, though he had never seen her before today. He had traveled a vast distance for her and had waited a lifetime. But from what he had seen already, she had been worth the journey and the wait.

Deeper into the forest she led him, and he marveled at her grace and agility as she glided among the feathery ferns, the tangled thickets, the thorny brambles. Shafts of sunlight broke through the branches of the trees overhead and lit her hair with a blue-black sheen. As he watched, the stranger likened her to one of the ravens flitting from limb to limb above them. She was as much a part of the forest as the birds, the trees, and the hares that rustled in the elderberry bushes on either side of the path.

But as they neared a small clearing in the trees, he sensed a change in her. Her body tensed as it had when she had stood before the council. With her hands clenched into fists she lifted her chin and walked straight ahead, her eyes focused in front of her. Something was obviously disturbing her. It seemed she had battles to fight, even here in the forest.

Off to the right, in the center of a ring of gnarled oaks, stood the object she was avoiding. The moment he saw it, a chill swept through him. In the small clearing was a pile of stones about waist-high, and from the middle of the mound rose a gray stone pillar, an ominous-looking obelisk with strange engravings chiseled into its timeworn, smoke-blackened surface.

From the top of the column dangled two heavy iron chains, and at the ends of the chains hung a pair of thick, rusted manacles.

The man knew this place. Somewhere deep in his spirit he recognized it, even as he had recognized the woman when he had first seen her standing before the council.

He hesitated; then, reaching a decision, he allowed her to go on alone. He couldn't leave the site, not until he knew its secrets.

As soon as she had disappeared among the trees, he climbed the pile of stones. Standing before the pillar, he closed his eyes and took a deep breath. Slowly, reverently, he lifted his right hand and laid his palm against the engraved surface.

In an instant his arm went numb to the shoulder. An icy shock coursed through his body as he absorbed the power that radiated from the stone. A flood of emotions and impressions engulfed him; unspeakable terror, unbearable pain that scorched and seared. He felt as though the flames of hell itself were consuming his body, and he smelled the rancid odor of burning hair and flesh. His hair. His flesh. Smoke, thick and suffocating, billowed around him, filling his lungs and stealing his breath. He heard the crowd's screams, mixed with the roar of the fire, and he knew they were crying out for his death, delighting in his agony. They wanted him to die . . . and he didn't know why.

Using all his strength, he pulled his hand away from the stone. Instantly the sensations were gone; the searing pain of the fire, the choking smoke, the mob's cries. The stranger stood for a long moment, fighting the rage that swept over him, robbing him of rational thought. The injustice of what he had just seen and felt convinced him, more than ever, that he had been summoned to this place to right a terrible wrong. Too many innocents had died at the hands of those whose power had so far remained uncontested.

He thought of the young woman standing in quiet defiance before the town council. He remembered her words about the miner children, her defense of her own mother and the other women with healing powers who had been murdered.

She faced an enormous challenge, this lady of the forest. And as he stood there beside the pillar, the core of her sorrow, he thanked the powers that had brought him to this place to stand with her against the evil that held the village of Hamelin captive.

He sensed the inherent courage of the woman and the strength that would be generated between the two of them. Working together, surely they could break those bonds of corruption, suspicion, and greed and set the children free.

Leisel walked by the stones as quickly as possible, without a sideways glance. But the stone pillar still singed her with the flames of a scalding, bitter memory.

She could never forget what had happened in that place, and yet she wouldn't allow herself to remember. Someday, she told herself, she would find the courage to face that memory. But until then, it would remain in the dark recesses of her mind, emerging only in her nightmares.

Leaving the path, she plunged into the thicket, toward the deepest part of the forest, the only place she felt safe these days. The villagers didn't come into the dark center of the forest. They said it was wicked, this place where the trees grew thickest, letting through only the occasional shaft of sunlight. Here the smell of decaying loam was the most pungent. The mosses grew a deeper shade of emerald, the ferns reached higher than Leisel's waist, and the bramble thorns were as long as her hand. No human sounds invaded this sylvan sanctuary; the only voices were those of the forest birds, the animals, and the rippling of the creek that flowed through the heart of the woods.

Leisel sat beside the edge of the creek, pulled off her slippers, and dangled her feet in the clear water. Closing her eyes, she allowed the serenity of the place to seep into her soul, easing the grip of fear that was clutching at her chest.

In spite of the peace of the forest, Leisel couldn't clear her mind of the faces of her accusers. Father Beck and Herr Schmidt wanted to see her dead, and they wouldn't stop until their vindictive yearning was satisfied. As she had many times before, Leisel thought back over the past six years, wondering what she had done to deserve their wrath. But, as always, she could find no answers.

The night Leisel's mother had died, Baron Schmidt had taken Leisel into his home at his wife's prompting. At the time he had paid her no more attention than he had paid his game hounds. All that had changed three years ago when her girl's body had blossomed into that of a woman's. Since then he had desired and despised her at the same moment.

His eyes would sweep her, then accuse her, as though it were somehow her fault that she had grown breasts, that her waist had narrowed and her hips had broadened.

His unwholesome interest had made Leisel's life miserable. She had quickly learned that the only way she could survive in the baron's household was to stay as far away from him as possible. But lately he had been making that more and more difficult to do. He followed her from room to room, making lewd suggestions under his breath, brushing his body against hers at every opportunity, and even grabbing at her breasts when they were alone in the kitchen.

Then there was Father Beck. The priest had harbored a special dislike and mistrust of Leisel since she could remember. Her earliest memory of him was a morning long ago when she was very young. She recalled standing on the porch of her cottage, hiding behind the skirt of her mother's tunic. The priest had poked her cheek with a bony finger as he questioned her mother. Although Leisel hadn't understood the entire conversation, she never had forgotten his accusation . . . something about her father being the devil. Her mother had answered the priest in a loud, harsh voice, one that Leisel had never heard her use before. And he had left. Even then Leisel had recognized the venom in the man and the enmity between him and Katrina Kistner. Leisel had sensed even then that this man would do her mother harm in the end.

Often Leisel had known that things were going to happen before they came to pass. Once she had dreamed that Goddard Wilheim, the town crier, would fall off the roof of his house and break both his legs. When it had happened, Katrina had warned her daughter not to mention her foresight. She had explained that some people might think Leisel had caused the calamity. Being able to see into the future was both a blessing and a curse, Katrina had said, and she had cautioned Leisel to take care when telling others what tomorrow held.

That day on the porch, Leisel had known that Father Beck would cause her mother's death. She had known but had been unable to do anything to prevent it.

Her mother. Leisel lifted her feet from the creek, scooped up handfuls of the sparkling water, and buried her face in the cool wetness, trying to remember her mother's green eyes, trying to forget how her beautiful black hair had turned to silver almost overnight. In the still water that pooled at her bare feet Leisel saw her own reflection, and for a moment she was astonished at how much she resembled her mother. When Father Beck and Baron Schmidt looked at her, did they see the young woman whom they had condemned to death? Perhaps this was why her mother's enemies had become her own.

Contemplating this possibility, Leisel rose and walked slowly away from the creek toward a gnarled tree stump that lay on its side, where it had fallen, lightning-struck, years before. Casting a cautious glance around her into the dark thicket, Leisel knelt beside the tree, thrust one hand into the log, and pulled out a small object wrapped in a red silk scarf. With loving care she untied the cloth, uncovering a leather-bound book.

Her hand trembled as she stared down at the book. Her mother's book. The journal and the red scarf were all that remained of the woman who had brought her into the world and nurtured her, the only evidence that she had existed. The journal was Leisel's only link with the one person who had ever loved her. Tears streaming down her face, she closed her eyes and clutched it to her breast. Touching the book wasn't as satisfying as cuddling in her mother's arms, but it was all she had left; Hamelin's town council had seen to that.

After several moments she opened her eyes and pressed

her lips against the soft leather. Then she removed her apron and tied it around the book. Carefully she replaced the bundle in the log.

Rising, she wove the scarf through her long hair, braiding it into the silver streak that flowed from her right temple. Feeling somewhat bolstered and rejuvenated, she lifted her chin and turned to leave, taking the path on which she had come.

In the thicket a shadow moved among the darker shadows, gliding through the brush, following the young woman but staying out of her sight. It trailed her, not as a hunter would stalk his prey but as an animal would track its young.

The shadow was the shape of a giant wolf. When the wolf passed through the occasional shafts of sunlight, its fur sparkled. Like silver.

Four

MONIKA WAS DYING. Leisel sensed the specter of imminent death as she looked down into the small, flushed face. There was nothing she could do to save her. Two days before, the girl's wound had become dark and foul-smelling, and she had lapsed into a fevered lethargy.

With Trudl's help, Leisel had moved Monika from the shed where the other children were housed to the stable where Leisel slept every night. In spite of Leisel's constant care, neither her poultices nor Helga's special ointments had reduced the swelling in the child's arm or abated her fever.

"Monika?" Leisel whispered as she bent over the little girl, applying the damp cloth to the child's forehead. For a moment the girl's eyelids fluttered open. But Leisel saw no light of recognition or awareness shining in Monika's round eyes. It was as though the child's spirit had flown from her body, leaving it as empty as a bird's nest once the chicks had gone.

Unable to look into the empty eyes that had sparkled with life only days before, Leisel glanced across the horse stall at Trudl. The plain young girl was huddled on a bale of hay, her knees drawn up to her chin, her lanky arms wrapped around her shins.

"Why doesn't she get better?" Trudl asked, her large, lashless eyes wide with pity and concern. "It's been ten days since the cave-in, since she was hurt. The others are better now." She swallowed and shuffled her feet in the straw. "They've recovered or—"

"Or they've died," Leisel supplied in a voice tinged with bitterness. She didn't want to make Trudl feel worse by reminding her of her father's transgressions, but since this morning's breakfast when the baron had announced that he intended to reopen the mine in one week, Leisel had scarcely been able to contain her rage.

She looked down at Monika's arm, swollen and dark with putrefaction. How could any man look on a child's suffering and allow it to happen again and again? Obviously the baron's only consideration was for his coin purse.

"Why should she get better?" Leisel asked, wetting the muslin rags in the horse's trough and applying them to the girl's face, arms, and legs. "If she gets well, your father will only send her back into the mines again. Most of the children who work in that dark pit would prefer to die."

Out of the corner of her eye Leisel saw Trudl shudder. Leisel wasn't sure if Trudl was reacting to her father's abuse of the pauper children, or if her dismay was caused by the six gray rats that scrambled from a feed bag that hung from the barn loft. The bottom of the sack had ripped open from the gnawing, and the grain had spilled onto the straw-covered floor.

"They're getting worse," Trudl said, nodding to the pile of hay where the rats had disappeared. Within moments nine more of the rodents scurried from under the straw and joined the others that were eating the grain. "A big rat attacked Frau Mitterheim's new baby in its cradle last evening. Father Beck says it's a plague, a sign of the last days before the end of the world."

"I'm not surprised that Father Beck would find some holy reason to explain the rats," Leisel said dryly, "when the true reason is obvious enough. If you kill all the cats, the rats abound."

No sooner had she spoken the words than Leisel heard a movement at the barn door. She turned to see the baron standing there, dressed only in his hose and a light tunic. "Is this blasphemy I hear?" he asked. An unpleasant smile creased his face, and his small eyes glimmered in the lantern light.

"I'm not questioning the acts of God himself," Leisel replied, rising to place herself between Schmidt and the injured child. "Only the actions of those who say they serve Him."

"I'd watch my tongue if I were you, girl," the baron said as he walked into the barn. His eyes passed over Monika, dismissing her without a moment's consideration. Then he saw his daughter huddled on the bale of straw, looking as though she wished she could curl into a ball so small that no one would find her.

"There you are, Trudl," he said, walking over to her. He picked up one of her thin brown braids and caressed it, and Trudl cringed as though the touch caused her pain. "I've been searching the house for you. Your mother's head is giving her misery once again, and she has retired to her bedchamber for the evening. I want you to keep me company."

As always, Leisel wondered at the fear that darkened Trudl's eyes whenever her father was present. There was something unwholesome about the way the baron looked at his daughter, something that made Leisel feel ill when she thought about it. She had suspicions, but she didn't dare put the thoughts to words, didn't dare name the sin of which she thought him guilty.

Trudl rose obediently, casting a helpless, sidelong look at Leisel, who simply stared down at her patient. She wanted to help Trudl, but how? The baron was too powerful, his grip on his family too tight. Leisel knew that he would clutch his daughter to him, squeezing until there was no life left in her.

As Leisel watched the two of them walk out the barn door, she realized that most of Trudl had died already. Like a tender violet crushed by a careless hand, the sweetness and the fragrance had gone out of her. Although her body was still whole, her eyes were as empty as Monika's. Leisel hated the baron for killing the children in his keeping . . . and for killing Trudl from the inside out.

"Hold on, *liebchen*," she said as she looked down at the child who shivered in the straw at her feet. "He murdered your mother, as he did mine. We're all that's left of the women who gave us life. We can't let him kill us, too. We have to fight him . . . for their sake."

Monika said nothing; she was obviously too weak for any response. Gathering the small, frail body into her arms, Leisel rocked the child gently until she had drifted into a deep sleep. Then Leisel laid her in the straw and covered her with her own threadbare blanket. Having done all she could for the little girl, Leisel walked over to the window, where she stood for a long time looking up at the night sky. The moon was just rising over the top of Koppelberg Mountain, spreading its silver light over the purple hills.

Leisel closed her eyes and listened for the song. Remembering her dream of a week ago, she tried to recall what she had found when she had run across the meadow toward the forest. Someone had been waiting there among the trees for her. Someone with strong arms that had enfolded her in a comforting embrace. Sometimes she felt he was very near, this moonlight lover whose song was so clear but whose face was still hidden in darkness. Tonight he felt very close. She could feel his arms around her . . . almost but not quite.

At first she thought he was a dream, this man who stood over her, his face in shadow, moonlight streaming over his body. Slowly Leisel sat up from the straw pallet where she had been sleeping beside Monika.

The man didn't move but simply stood before her. Although she couldn't see his face, she instinctively knew that he was looking down at her.

He was a large man, tall and slender, and dressed in a manner of clothing unlike any she had ever seen before. He wore hose, but his were tighter than those worn by the men in Hamelin, and they clearly outlined the heavy muscles in his thighs. Instead of lightweight slippers he wore doeskin boots that rose high on his thighs. His tunic was a finer fabric than she had ever seen. It had a sheen to it, like polished silver, and there was ornate embroidery around the neckline and hem. His waist was girded with a leather belt from which hung a short sword. On its hilt was a jeweled crest in the shape of a stag's head.

But it was his cloak that held her attention. She had never seen such a garment before, not even on the peddlers or tradesmen who traveled through the village. This cloak was a hundred different colors, woven into a patchwork of hues that shimmered and danced in the moonlight. Fastened at his throat with a silver brooch, the cape hung from his broad shoulders to the heels of his boots.

He looked like a king, a wandering spirit. *Or maybe the devil himself,* Leisel thought with a shudder. Father Beck had said that the devil could make himself beautiful so that you couldn't recognize his evil.

"Who are you?" she whispered.

He said nothing but moved fully into the moonlight so that she could see his features. It was a handsome face, foreign and yet familiar to her. His hair glittered, golden in the silver light, and as Leisel looked up at him, her heart pulsing in her throat, it occurred to her that no man could be so beautiful. He had to be a spirit, after all.

"Did the moon send you?" she asked, knowing that she

could die for even speaking such heresy but sensing that he would understand.

"I'm a friend," he said.

Leisel was surprised that she recognized his voice, as well. It was deep and gentle, like the roar of thunder mixed with soft rain.

"Why are you here?"

"I've come to help," he said, moving closer to her.

In that moment Leisel didn't know what to do. Part of her wanted to run to him, to put her arms around him and feel him embrace her, as though they had both been waiting a lifetime to touch. The other part of her wanted to flee, to run out of the barn and away from the power that she felt radiating from this man. It was the same power that her mother had exuded. The same power that Leisel had within herself; it could cause her to be killed, as it had her mother.

"What can I do for you, my lady?" he asked. She heard the humility in his words, the sincere desire to serve. How could this be? This man who looked like a king offering to be her servant?

"Simply ask me what you will," he said, "and it will be done."

Ask anything? Surely he didn't mean what he was saying. Leisel's eyes searched the man's and saw an openness that took her aback. Perhaps he had come to help her, after all.

"What would you have me do?" he asked again as he took a step closer to her.

Take me away from this place, she thought. *Take me to a far-away land where those around me don't stare at me with hungry eyes. Take me to a place where I don't have to be afraid of the power inside me. A place that isn't haunted by the horrors of the past.*

But Leisel didn't ask for any of these things. Instead she looked down at the child who slept fitfully on the straw beside her, the child Leisel had taken under her wing the night Monika's mother had been burned at the stake.

"Make her well," she said. "Please help me save her life."

Without hesitation he walked over to the girl and knelt on one knee beside her. With gentle hands he touched the child's swollen arm. "What happened to her?" he asked, though Leisel had an inexplicable feeling that he already knew.

"She worked in the mine at Koppelberg Mountain. The tunnel collapsed, and many of the children were hurt. Some of them died."

He said nothing as his hands moved over the girl's limbs, checking for more injuries. Then he brushed the auburn curls away from her flushed face with his fingertips. "There's poison in her arm," he said, "and it's spreading. That's why she is fevered. Her body is trying to burn the poison out of her, but it needs help."

"Can you save her?" Somehow Leisel believed that he could, this man who had stepped out of the moon and into her world.

He reached into the haversack that he had dropped into the straw and pulled out a leather pouch. "I can try."

Helping when she could, Leisel watched as he fashioned a poultice from some strange herbs, a foul-smelling yellow powder, and a liquid, which he poured from a pewter flask that hung on his belt. With skill that amazed her, he quickly bound the arm.

"That will help draw the poisons from her body," he said, "and this will ease her pain." He pulled another flask from inside his full, banded sleeve and coaxed a few drops between the child's lips.

"Will she recover?" Leisel tucked the tattered blanket around Monika's shoulders.

"Why does she matter so much to you?" he asked, watching her closely. "Is she your sister?"

Leisel's lips tilted in a bitter smile. "Some say that we're half sisters. We had different mothers. This village murdered them both. But many in Hamelin say we share the same father."

"And who do they say sired you and this child?"

"The devil. They say we're daughters of Lucifer himself."

At first he remained silent as his eyes traveled over her face, her body, her hair, lingering on the silver streak twined with the red scarf. "You're a beautiful woman," he said finally, "and strong. There are those who envy beauty and fear strength. That's why they destroyed your mother. They'll try to destroy you in the end."

Leisel nodded, a somber expression on her pretty face. "I know. But for tonight it isn't me who's in danger. It's this child." She motioned toward the sleeping Monika and asked again, "Will she live?"

"If she wants to recover, she'll live. If she doesn't . . ." He shrugged.

"She doesn't want to go back into the mine." Leisel looked down at the white, pinched face.

A flash of anger lit the man's eyes, like a bolt of lightning across the night sky. But the look was gone just as quickly. "Tell her she won't have to go back into the mine," he said.

Leisel shook her head. "I can't lie to her. She *will* have to go. They all have to return."

The man studied Monika for a long moment. When he looked up at Leisel, something in his eyes made her shiver. This man would be a powerful ally, but she wouldn't want him for a foe.

"The children will be free," he said. "That much I promise you. And this one, the one you love, she'll never go into the mine again. You can tell her that, knowing you speak the truth."

She believed him. She didn't know why, but instinctively she sensed that this man would never make a promise to her that he couldn't keep.

A formidable power kept the children in the mines: the power of greed, the baron's greed, the town's greed. But there was an air of authority about this stranger that she had never witnessed in anyone, not even in the noble councilmen of Hamelin. If anyone could help her, help the children, it was this man who wore a cloak of a thousand colors and carried the moonlight in his hair.

Sitting down on the straw beside Monika, Leisel stroked the child's forehead and said, "Rest, *liebchen*. Rest and heal yourself. Soon you'll be well. You'll feel the sun on your face and the wind in your hair. And there will be no more digging in the darkness, I promise." She looked up into the man's pale blue eyes and felt his strength and conviction. "*We* promise."

At the sound of her voice Monika seemed to relax. She drew a shuddering sigh, and some of the shadows of pain faded from her small face. Leisel felt the tightness in her chest began to loosen just a bit, a constriction that she had experienced since the night when she had first sensed the cave-in. She, too, drew a deep breath of relief. Perhaps there was hope for the children, after all.

The man reached beneath his cloak and pulled out a thin silver object. At first Leisel thought that it was some kind of wand. Then she saw that it was a pipe—a musical pipe.

To her surprise and delight he sat down in the straw beside Monika, his long legs crossed before him. He said nothing more but lifted the pipe to his lips and began to play.

The first notes grabbed at Leisel's heart and held it. She shivered as the music spilled over her and through her, music she recognized in the deepest, most hidden part of her heart. Music that she had never heard before, a song that she had always known. It was the moon's song. Clear, shimmering, light, and delicate as moonbeams. A haunting song that made her want to laugh and weep in the same moment.

"It's beautiful," she whispered. And she thought he heard her, because his eyes glimmered briefly.

As he continued to play, a peace stole over Leisel's heart and mind, a peace so profound that she lay down beside Monika and closed her eyes to rest them for a moment. But in less than a minute she had drifted into a deep sleep, a sleep rich with dreams.

In the morning when she awoke, the silver moon was gone, and golden sunlight was streaming through the stable windows.

Monika's fever had broken. Her arm was less swollen.

And the piper was gone.

Five

THE RATS WERE worse—much worse. When Leisel opened the door to the Schmidts' kitchen she saw more than a dozen scurrying for cover. Six of the larger, bolder ones stayed behind, ignoring her presence as they dipped their muzzles into the wheels of cheese and tugged at the bags of barley stored beneath the bread table.

When flapping her apron at them didn't work, Leisel took a broom from the corner and chased them out the door.

Several minutes later the baron walked into the room, and Leisel wished she could chase the human vermin away as quickly as the rodents.

"God in heaven, they're everywhere," he swore, his plump face flushed with irritation. "If I find out that you're behind this plague, girl, I swear I'll pour a ladle of melted fat over you and hold a torch to you myself."

Leisel swallowed the fear that his threat evoked and calmly continued to cut away the tooth-pocked edges from the block of cheese. "Why should I welcome the rats?" she asked. "They make my life as unpleasant as everyone else's."

"I doubt that. This very morning Trudl found a nest of the miserable creatures in her favorite hat. She's been weeping all morning, and nothing her mother or I do will console her."

Something in his words, his tone, didn't ring true. Leisel had known Trudl all her life, and if the girl was crying inconsolably this morning, it had to be more than a nest of rats that had caused her tears.

"This town has had quite enough calamities," he said as he moved around the kitchen, picking at bits of bread, cheese, and a joint of meat from the pot that simmered perpetually over the fire. "If anything else happens, you'll certainly be held responsible. The town is already crying out for vengeance against you, girl, devil's daughter that you are. We know where you learned the evil you practice . . . from your witch of a mother. I suppose you know, my goodwill is all that stands between you and a very unpleasant death. I hope you realize that."

"I realize that my life depends on you," she said with a bitterness that he didn't seem to notice.

He moved closer to her, so close that she could smell the cloying scent of the perfume he wore, which could not mask an even stronger smell, that of an unwashed, unhealthy body. Desperate to move away from him, she walked over to the bread table and began kneading the dough that had been resting there. He followed her, and placing his hands on the table on either side of her hips, he pinned her within his arms.

"If you know that your life depends on me, perhaps you'd better start acting that way." His breath was sour against her face, and she had to fight the urge to shove him away.

"I cook your meals," she said, more calmly than she felt. "And I clean your house. I'm handmaiden to your daughter. Surely that's enough to repay you for your kindness to me."

"I'll decide what payment I require," he said, lowering his face to hers.

Revulsion surged through her and she turned her cheek to him. "Please," she whispered, "please don't."

"Papa . . ."

They turned to see Trudl standing in the kitchen door, her lashless eyes red and swollen, her face tear-streaked.

"What is it, Trudl?" the baron asked, obviously irritated to be interrupted.

"It's Mama. Her head is hurting again. Shall I fetch the blood-letter?" As Trudl addressed her father, her eyes darted back and forth between Leisel and the baron, and indignation reddened her pallid cheeks. Leisel felt a flush of guilt but wasn't sure why. After all, she certainly wasn't choosing to be the object of the baron's depraved interest.

"No, you'll not summon the blood-letter again," he said as he strolled over to the fireplace and lifted a flask of wine from its iron hook on the mantel. "He was just here last evening, and the man charges dearly for the honor of his presence. I can't afford to have him take up permanent abode here, now can I? Tell your dear mother she'll just have to suffer through this time."

He lifted the flask and took a long draft, then his eyes raked Leisel's body in openly lecherous appraisal. Recently he had become more and more blatant about his unwholesome desires, Leisel noted with concern. He no longer seemed to care if his family knew his intentions. Leisel realized that her situation here in the Schmidt household was becoming more precarious each day.

Throwing the empty flask at Leisel's feet, he turned and stomped across the flagstone floor toward the door, mumbling something about women and their damned female weaknesses.

Leisel watched Trudl's eyes as the baron swept past her, and the hostility that Leisel saw on her young friend's face chilled her. For as long as Leisel had known her, Trudl's countenance had registered only fear. The girl had kept her anger suppressed, her eyes averted, her head tucked. But lately Leisel had been noticing a subtle difference in the way Trudl reacted to her father. As soon has his back was turned, she would shoot him a baleful glance that left no doubt about the depth of her hostility.

In one way Leisel was pleased to see her friend finally display some courage through silent defiance. On the other hand, Leisel was afraid for the girl. Leisel knew instinctively that the baron's will was much stronger than his daughter's. In the end he would win. If the day ever came that Trudl showed her father the magnitude of her wrath, her health—perhaps even her life—would be in jeopardy.

The piper moved quietly through the moonlit forest, the soft leather of his thigh-high boots making no sound on the cushion of the forest loam. His stride was confident, as though he knew the lay of the land, the position of every rock and tree. It was the step of a hunter, silent but sure.

But this time he wasn't stalking prey; he was searching. He had to find her, to see her. Even if he didn't speak to her, he had to reaffirm that she was truly as beautiful as he remembered.

Ahead, he could hear the sound of the creek that divided the woods north to south. He sensed that she would be there in her forest sanctuary; he knew somehow that she was nearby, so close that he could almost touch her with his spirit.

When he reached the glen, he stayed inside the shelter of the trees. His sharp eye caught a movement to his right, and he turned to see her standing beside the river. Her face was toward him, her head bowed, her long hair covering her features like a glimmering black curtain. His hands ached to touch that softness, to feel it wrap around his fingers, around his neck, to feel it trail across his bare chest.

As he watched, she slowly began to slip out of her apron, chemise, and skirts, letting the garments drop to the ground. His breath caught in his throat as her body was revealed to him. He felt guilty for watching. He knew that he should turn and go back the way he had come and forget what he had seen. But he couldn't. She was the most beautiful woman his eyes had ever beheld, and he was starved for the sight of her.

He was close enough to see the swell of her breasts, high, firm, and youthful, yet heavy like a woman's. The curve of her waist fascinated him. Her hips were full, wide enough for childbearing, he noted with satisfaction. Her skin glowed in the moonlight, and he reveled in the sight of such perfection. He would make her his. He vowed that someday soon he would hold her in his arms and touch that loveliness.

But when she turned her back to him and walked into the water, he gasped. All thoughts of possessing her fled and his desire turned to rage. Even from this distance he could see the scars, the crisscrossing that marred the perfection of her body. He had seen enough of life to know what had caused those scars. She had been whipped. Viciously.

He remembered the pile of stones, not far away, and the pain he had felt when laying his hand on the pillar. Pity and compassion welled up in his chest. In that moment he wanted nothing more than to take her in his arms, to touch those scars and wipe them away. He thought of how this woman had touched the little girl in the barn with such loving kindness, a kindness that healed even the deepest scars. And he wanted to heal hers.

Unable to control the fury and anguish that tore through him, he turned and plunged back into the forest. He ran until he could run no more, then he fell to his knees, his hand gripping the hilt of his sword.

He wanted to heal her, but more than anything else, in that moment he wanted to kill the man who had laid that whip across her back. And he swore, there on his knees, that he would.

· · ·

The river's cool waters had soothed her body but not her mind. Leisel lay on her pallet, tossing fitfully as she stared through the stable window at the moon. Beside her lay Monika, her breath soft and even. She slept peacefully, as only a child can. For a moment Leisel envied the girl. Then she thought of the mine and was ashamed.

Memories of her mother had dominated Leisel's thoughts tonight, and the recollections evoked strong and varied emotions. In the middle of a sun-warmed meadow her mother had shown her how to make a daisy chain for her hair. Lying on their backs in the fragrant grass, they had listened for the cuckoo and tried to imitate its cry, giggling helplessly all the while.

With her mother's arms around her, Leisel had felt safe. And as she lay there on the pallet and remembered, Leisel was able to recapture the feeling that all was right in her world. But the sensation was fleeting. Her mother was dead. Leisel was a woman herself now, and would never again know that warm feeling of safety, of protection. She was a woman alone, with only her own strength and wit to keep her alive.

Hate was the color red, swirling around her. Crimson. Blood. Fire. She could hear the crowd, familiar voices, voices she heard everyday in the cobbled streets and dark shops of the village. But the voices were different tonight, strained and high-pitched as they screamed, "Witch! Witch!"

Hands held her tightly, fingers clawing at her, nails sinking into her flesh. One woman grabbed a handful of her hair and forced her to look . . . to look at the red, the blood and the fire.

"Mother!" she cried, and tried to close her eyes, tried to blot out the sight that was burning into her eyes, her heart.

One of the men who was holding her struck her hard across the face. "Open your eyes, girl," he said. "Look and see what happens to those who work the devil's magic."

She looked. And the horrid scene before her eyes branded her memory with unforgettable, searing pain.

The young woman was tied to the stone pillar, her slender body sagging against the chains that held her captive. Her dress hung in shreds, nearly torn from her body by the mob. Her left arm dangled at her side while blood poured from the ragged stump where her hand had been severed. Although her long hair fell over her face it could not hide her agony, her torment, as she writhed and twisted against her bonds. Her head lolled from side to side as she moaned and cried weakly for someone in the crowd to help her.

In answer to her pleas the mob's frenzy escalated and they gathered yet more knots of wood and branches and threw the fuel on the fire. The flames caught and leapt, hotter and higher. The village children imitated their elders, scurrying around the edge of the fire that rose in a glowing circle around the woman. The children were shrieking, almost the same sound as when they were at play but with an underlying note of hysteria.

As though from afar, Leisel heard the screams of the children—some of them her playmates—and wondered why they would want to kill her mother. Why were they doing this? Didn't they know that her mother was good, that she helped people, that she made daisy chains in the meadow?

Leisel felt the scorching heat on her face, making her skin crawl. The wind caught the smoke and blew it toward the crowd. She gasped as the acrid smell stung her throat and lungs.

"Burn! Burn! Burn!" The voices were louder now.

But not loud enough to cover the screams of the woman as the circle of flames closed and enveloped her. Leisel tried to put her hands over her ears, but once again rough hands pulled them away.

"Listen!" shouted a voice in her ear. "Listen to the screams of the devil's bitch."

She looked up into the small-piggish eyes in the round face that was flushed red from the heat of the fire, and Leisel knew that she would hate Baron Schmidt for the rest of her life. If she had been bigger and stronger, if she were a man, she would have killed him right then, and jumped up on that pile of stones and torn those chains from around her mother and . . .

But it didn't matter. Leisel wasn't a man. And there wasn't a man or woman in the crowd who would save her mother. They were all screaming and chanting and watching while she burned to death. They wanted her to die because they hated her. The little girl, watching helplessly at the edge of the fire, cried out again and again the one word that would echo through her heart and mind for years to come: "Why? Why? Why?"

Leisel woke with a start. The moon had dipped behind Koppelberg Mountain and the stable was dark. She shivered and moved closer to the sleeping Monika, seeking the warmth and solace her small body offered. Though the dream had vanished, its aftermath had left her shaken.

Since that night so long ago, Leisel had learned more about people and their fears, and she now had the answer to her question. Her mother had died because she was different. In the village of Hamelin, anyone who was different was feared, and therefore hated and considered evil.

A new revelation swept over Leisel, adding to the sense of darkness and oppression that was closing in around her. She was like her mother; she was different. Sometimes she dreamed things that later came true. Sometimes she knew what someone was going to say a moment before he spoke. The minute she walked into a cottage she could tell if the people who lived there were happy or lived together in misery.

Once, she had passed over a bridge with her mother and had become violently ill. Her mother had told her that several years before, four young women had been thrown from that bridge and drowned because they had been accused of dancing at the crossroads at midnight to celebrate the coming of spring.

At times Leisel could see deeper into someone's heart than she wanted to, than they wanted her to. And she suspected that was the most dangerous difference of all. That was why they hated her. They were afraid she could see inside them and glimpse their darkest secrets, those things they hated about themselves.

Too unnerved to go back to sleep, Leisel lay awake the rest of the night. She was afraid she might dream again, afraid she would look up at that young woman being consumed by fire and see her own face.

Six

LEISEL HURRIED THROUGH the village streets, dodging the wagons laden with summer vegetables and fruits, caged fowl, and grains. Traders barked their wares from the corners where they had set up stands displaying lengths of linen and wool. From the poles that supported their stalls, bright ribbons fluttered in the breeze.

One of the merchants smiled as Leisel passed him, giving her the benefit of a grin that lacked all of its teeth but radiated warmth nevertheless.

"*Guten Morgen, Fraulein,*" he greeted her, beckoning her toward his display. "I have ribbons for your hair. Ah, you have a scarf already. Well, never mind, I have a bright blue ribbon right here for that lovely throat of yours."

"I have no money," she said, shyly returning his smile. She was unaccustomed to having anyone speak to her on the street. But then, this man wouldn't be flirting with her if he were from Hamelin, if he knew her reputation. As one of the many peddlers who passed through the busy trading village of Hamelin every day, this man didn't know that she was an outcast, shunned by all decent people.

"You don't need money, my pretty lady," he said, holding out the blue ribbon to her and pointing to his cheek. "One small kiss from your sweet lips and the ribbon will be yours."

She smiled and shook her head. Any other time she might have been tempted. The peddler was kind, and kindness was so seldom extended toward her that she welcomed friendship, even if it was offered by a stranger. But this morning she had no time for such things. She had errands to run for her mistress, Baroness Schmidt, and a flock of pauper children who needed their bandages changed and their spirits soothed.

Hurrying past him, she shifted her heavy basket to her other arm and quickened her steps. Inside the basket was the baron's midday meal; a pot of cheese, a round of bread, some apples, and a flask of wine. She mustn't be late with his meal. Food was even more important to the baron than his money.

She passed a knot of children gathered around the corpse of a small dog. The animal had been killed by a particularly aggressive pack of rats.

"Shh," whispered one of the boys, nodding in Leisel's direction. "It's the witch. My papa says she's the one who brought the rats."

"And she caused the mine to fall, too," muttered one of his playmates, an innocent-looking girl with round blue eyes and several of the peddler's ribbons twisted in her blond curls.

"Don't look into her eyes," the boy admonished the others. "She can turn you into a rat, you know. My mama says so."

"Or worse yet, she'll steal your soul and sell it to the devil," added the oldest boy, a child whom Leisel had seen following at Father Beck's heels lately.

The joy of the summer morning vanished for Leisel, and she felt the darkness closing in around her once more. If the citizens of Hamelin chose to believe the worst about her without evidence of her guilt, why did they have to pass their hatred on to their children? If ignorance was handed down, generation after generation, where would it end?

Leisel tried to ignore their murmurings as she passed, her eyes straight ahead on her destination, the town hall. As she neared the place she saw that a crowd had gathered outside the front door of the building. Her heart caught in her throat as she remembered the mob in her dream the night before. This crowd was agitated, too, but it was a different kind of anger, a controlled indignation, not the frenzied mania of her dream.

Leisel slipped around the building and entered through the back door. Inside, she found the baron and the other council members seated at the large oak trestle table, facing a roomful of angry villagers. For once the baron didn't look interested in his food basket. He didn't even notice her as she quietly waited in the corner of the room.

"We can't bear it anymore!" shouted Klaus Niklaus, raising his arms to the ceiling to show his distress. The miller's abrupt gesture sent clouds of flour swirling through the air. "The rats have taken over the village. You must do something!"

"Yes," said Rolf Gunter, the brawny cooper. "What do you think we're paying you for, to sit here and watch the rats carry us all away?"

"And what do you propose we do about this?" The baron leaned back on his bench, his fingers interlaced atop his ample belly.

The crowd hummed as suggestions flew around the room.

"Hire someone to kill them," someone said. "Pay him for every tail he collects."

"A rat slayer?" The baron raised one eyebrow in a sarcastic smirk. "And who among you has ever heard of such a man?"

"Bring in an army of cats," said Helga. "We can find more than enough in Hanover where they weren't foolish enough to kill them all."

Leisel cringed to hear Helga speak her mind so bluntly before the council. Had she no fear for her own safety? Leisel had often wondered how Helga had escaped the "purging" fires. Perhaps because she was so old and so ugly that no one cared.

"We'll have no more cats in Hamelin," Father Beck said, lifting his crooked nose a bit higher. "Bringing witches' familiars among us is only inviting sin, and we have enough such problems already."

He cast a sideways glance at Leisel, and more than two dozen eyes turned her way. In that moment she wished she could change her shape into that of a rat and scurry into a hole in the wall. After all, she was a witch, wasn't she? And witches were supposed to be able to change themselves into any of the "unclean" animals.

"Find out what's causing this!" the candle maker said. He, too, tossed an accusing look in Leisel's direction. "Or *who* is causing it. You're our governing council, and it's in your hands to do something."

Leisel could feel the hostility rising around her in waves. And she knew better than anyone how powerful that hate could be.

Summoning her courage, she lifted her chin and returned their stares, eye to eye. It was the wrong thing to do—she could feel it—but she wasn't going to cower. She had seen Monika's mother cower. Only three years ago that young woman had pleaded her innocence, begged for her life, cried for mercy. But she had met the same fate as Leisel's mother.

Leisel suspected that it would make no difference in the end whether she stood tall or bowed her knee. At least she would deny them the satisfaction of breaking her spirit or tarnishing her dignity. If she must die, it would be on her feet.

Just when she thought the villagers' eyes would scorch her, their attention was diverted. Someone was passing through the crowd, striding from the back of the room to the front. Like trees bending before a strong wind, people stepped aside and allowed the man to pass. Dressed in strangely regal clothes, he was a head taller than the tallest villager.

Leisel caught her breath. It was the strange man from the barn. The piper.

Once, years before, she had seen a white stag moving through the forest, its carriage proud, its movements fluid, its muscles rippling in the early-morning light. This man reminded her of the stag, graceful in form and motion. Both deer and man were beautifully male.

The room buzzed with curious whispers.

"Who is he?"

"Such odd clothes. Where is he from?"

"Look at his sword. There are jewels in its hilt!"

The piper walked up to the council's table and stood before it, his arms crossed over his broad chest, his cloak thrown back over his shoulders.

His pale blue eyes swept the hall, pausing on Leisel. He smiled, and the simple gesture told her she wasn't alone in this room full of hungry eyes.

He turned back to the table and scrutinized the council members. Though he seemed unimpressed by most, his eyes lingered on the baron. For a long, tense moment the two men stared at each other, a peculiar enmity radiating between them, as though they were old foes rather than strangers who had just met.

"Would you like to address this honorable council, sir?" the baron said, breaking the silence at last.

At the word *honorable* the piper's lips curled in one corner. Contempt shone in his eyes as he glanced over the baron's and Father Beck's fine wool robes.

"I understand you're being visited by a pestilence," he replied.

Laughter rippled through the crowd as three large rats scrambled the length of the table, nearly running over the toes of the baron's pigskin slippers. "That is obvious, I should think," Herr Schmidt replied.

Leisel watched the piper carefully, noting how his right hand rested on the jeweled hilt of his sword.

"I can rid these good people of their plague," he said. His voice was deep and resonant as it vibrated through the council chamber.

There was a collective drawing of breath, but no one spoke.

"And how would you accomplish this feat?"asked Father Beck in his most priestly tone. "Would you use holy means or evil?"

"Any act can be judged good or evil, depending upon how its results affect others. If I take away the misery of these people, my actions can only be called good, I should think." His words were even, his tone benign, but his eyes flashed with suppressed anger. Leisel wondered if the other villagers noticed the depth of his passion. Did the people of Hamelin feel the power radiating out of this man?

She looked around the room at the crowd that had been so agitated before. They were all staring at the stranger, their mouths gaping, their eyes wide, mesmerized by the spell he cast.

"Why should we trust that you can do such a thing?" the baron asked. "I, for one, don't believe that you can."

"You need not trust me," he said. "Only watch and believe your own eyes when it comes to pass. If a single rat remains in Hamelin village, you owe me not a penny."

The baron lifted one shaggy eyebrow. "Pay? And what sum would you be paid for this service, my good fellow? Twenty guilders? Thirty?"

"The sum I demand is not in coin, but in human life."

"What do you mean?"

The piper smiled, like a warrior who was about to win a battle and was already enjoying the victory. "If I rid Hamelin of its rats, you must close the Koppelberg Mountain mine. And it is to remain closed forever."

For the first time since the stranger had entered the room, the villagers began chattering among themselves.

"He doesn't want money?" the miller exclaimed, shaking his head in wonder. "What kind of man refuses to be paid in gold?"

"Perhaps a man who has gold enough," said the cooper, eyeing the stranger's clothing and jeweled sword.

Old Helga smiled her toothless grin and added, "Or a man who cares more about children than he cares for gold."

The baron stared up at the man who towered before his council table. His cheeks flushed a deep scarlet, and his dewlaps trembled as he said, "That, sir, is impossible. You must accept your payment in coin—or not at all."

The stranger shrugged his broad shoulders. "Then you will have the rats among you for a very long time. Either way, it matters naught to me."

He turned and started to walk out of the room, but Helga stepped in front of him, blocking his path. "Listen to him!" she said, her black eyes flashing in her wrinkled face.

"Yes, close the mine!" several of them shouted.

"Do whatever he says," Gretel, the cooper's wife said. "The rats killed my children's dog this morning. Something must be done."

Baron Schmidt sprang to his feet and clutched his robe protectively around his girth. "But this is foolishness. How can he get rid of the rats? He's lying. There are thousands of them. No single man could perform such a task."

"If he fails, you needn't close the mine," said Lambert, the candle maker. "What do you have to lose?"

Leisel cringed. She knew exactly what the baron had to lose—the only thing that really mattered to him—his fortune, made on the bent backs of pauper children.

The baron brought his fist down on the table with a heavy thud, and several of his fellow councilmen flinched. "Do you know what would happen to this village if I were to shut the mine down permanently?" he said. "Do you realize how much revenue that mine brings into this town?"

"It doesn't matter how much money we have if our children are being eaten alive in their cradles," said Helga.

The piper said nothing, just stood there expressionless as he listened to the villagers argue. Leisel felt herself reaching out to him, lending her support. And in that moment he turned and looked at her. There was something between her and this strange man with hair the color of the sun and eyes like a morning sky. It felt like the bond she had experienced with her mother, only stronger. Much stronger.

"Let him try," Helga said as she shuffled on stiff limbs to stand beside the piper. "What can be the harm in letting him try?"

Leisel watched as the baron looked from the stranger to the villagers and back. Then he glanced down the table at Father Beck, who wore a noncommittal look on his pinched face. For perhaps the first time in his life, Baron Schmidt stood at odds with his people. For years he had kept them under his fist. Only a plague like the rats could have brought them to mutiny.

Leisel enjoyed a moment of revenge as she watched Baron Schmidt face the hostile crowd. Would he bend to the will of the common people because of the power of their numbers and the depth of their desperation?

The baron turned to the piper, his jaw set, his little porcine eyes blazing. "I suspect that you're a scoundrel, with nothing more in mind than to rob this village. But for some reason these people believe in you, so I must give you the chance. If the rats are gone by sundown tomorrow, I'll do as you wish."

"You'll close the mine?" The piper's words were slow and deliberate.

"That's what I said," the baron snapped.

"And it will remain closed forever?"

"If every single rat is gone. If even one remains, the mine will continue to operate."

The handsome stranger smiled and bowed low to the council. "Then I bid you good day, gentlemen," he said. "Tomorrow morning at dawn, I'll lead every rat, its brother, mother, and cousin, out of your village. Until then, God be with you."

With one last look at Leisel, he turned and swept out of the room. Once again, the villagers stepped aside and let him pass. Leisel noticed with amused satisfaction that they were careful not even to allow his cloak to brush against them. The citizens of Hamelin were terrified of anyone who was different, and this man wasn't like anyone who had ever walked among them.

No one said anything for a long moment after he left. The silence was heavy with wonder about this strange man who had come and gone, leaving a powerful sense of himself behind.

Finally Baron Schmidt cleared his throat and said, "He won't be able to do it. You'll all see. No man can do such a thing."

"That's true," Father Beck said, nodding his head. "And if he does, it will be through the power of the devil. That much is certain."

The priest turned to Baron Schmidt, and the look that passed between them chilled Leisel's blood. It seemed to her that Father Beck was assuring the baron he couldn't lose this gamble. If the stranger failed, the mine would remain open and the townspeople made fools. If he succeeded, the town council would condemn him to death for practicing witch-craft. And the mine would stay open.

Leisel's heart twisted as she realized that the only one who would lose was the piper. And the price might be his life.

Trudl sat on the side of her bed, staring down at her

hands, which were folded in her lap. Leisel stood beside her, combing the girl's thin brown hair with a comb carved from a piece of pine. Leisel had made the comb herself and given it to Trudl as a gift three years before. The oil from the pine made the girl's drab hair glisten like a bird's wing. Trudl was a sparrow, small, colorless, easily discounted by those around her.

Sometimes Leisel thought that she was the only one who loved Trudl, who could see past the lashless eyes into the soul of a girl who wanted so badly to love and be loved. Besides Leisel, no one in Trudl's world recognized her wounded heart or its capacity for affection.

Every night when Leisel combed Trudl's hair, they talked about what had happened in their respective worlds that day. Often Leisel thought that her life, hard as it was, was more interesting and fulfilling than Trudl's. At least Leisel had her duties to the Schmidts to keep her busy, besides her time spent with the miner children. Trudl spent her days doing needlepoint, as the daughter of a nobleman should, sewing a wedding trousseau that would probably never be worn; in spite of the baron's wealth, there wasn't one suitor knocking at the door. It was no secret that Trudl Schmidt was considered to be painfully ugly by the town's eligible young men. They muttered insults to her back as she passed through the village, calling her "guinea legs" and "hawk beak," referring to her thinness and crooked nose.

Knowing how it felt to be an outcast, Leisel tried to show affection to Trudl whenever possible. When she combed her hair, she tried to do it as gently as possible, and tonight she was being even more careful than usual because Trudl was having one of her headaches. Like her mother, Trudl was afflicted with this recurrent malady, and Leisel had noticed that lately the pains had become more frequent and more intense.

"Do you think he can do it?" Trudl asked, twisting her

hands nervously in her lap. Leisel had noticed her doing that a lot lately.

"Who?"

"The man with the strange clothes. Do you think he can get rid of the rats?"

"I think he will," Leisel replied, surprised at the conviction in her own voice. For some reason she could believe anything of this man.

"I hope so," Trudl said with a sigh. "Then my father will have to close the mine, and the little ones won't have to go down into that terrible place ever again."

Leisel heard the hope and compassion in Trudl's voice and loved her for it. Some people were just born good, it seemed, with a heart that felt others' pain. Leisel marveled at the depth of Trudl's concern for a group of children whom she didn't know and had seldom even seen. Only this morning Trudl had convinced the baroness to send some hams and churns of butter to the children to aid their recovery. The last thing Leisel wanted to do was to crush Trudl's optimism by telling her that her father would probably find some way to keep the mine open, even if the piper were to rid the town of its plague.

"But how will he catch all the rats," Trudl asked, "let alone kill them?"

Leisel stopped combing for a moment as both girls listened to the scratching of rats' feet scrambling across the rafters overhead.

"I don't know." Leisel resumed her grooming. "But I know that Monika was nearly dead and he brought her back to life. He fashioned a poultice, gave her something to drink from his flask, and played a song for her on his pipe. Since that night she's grown stronger and stronger. I don't know how he'll get rid of the rats. But if he says he will, I believe him."

Leisel laid the comb aside and passed her fingertips over Trudl's temples. "Is it hurting very bad tonight?"

Trudl nodded gingerly. "Very bad."

Gently Leisel massaged her friend's head, feeling a power in her hands, a power that she could somehow impart to Trudl. She couldn't explain it, but she could feel some of her strength flowing from her own body into Trudl's—a healing strength—and she was glad to be able to impart this vitality to someone she loved.

"What are you doing?" Trudl asked, her voice weak from the pain.

"I'm not sure," she said. "But it feels like the right thing to do. The healing thing. And my mother always told me that if it feels like the right thing to do, deep down inside, then it probably is."

Trudl cringed slightly. "Your mother taught you?" she asked cautiously. "You aren't putting a witch's spell on me, are you?"

Leisel's heart panged, but she swallowed her pain. "No, of course not. I wouldn't hurt you. You know that."

"But my father says you're a witch. That you brought the rats to Hamelin to punish us for burning your mother at the stake."

"Your father says a lot of things that aren't true. I'm just surprised that you would listen to him. You know me. Do you think I'd deliberately do evil to anyone? Do you think I'd consort with the devil?"

"No, I suppose not. But sometimes I do wonder if . . ."

Leisel took her hands and squeezed them between her own. They were cold. Even in summer, Trudl's hands were always cold. "You can say anything to me."

"Sometimes I've wondered if you consort with my father. I've seen the way he looks at you. I've heard the things he's said to you. And I wonder if he's ever . . . if you've ever . . ."

Leisel drew a deep breath. "No, Trudl. I've never allowed him to get that close to me. To be honest, he's tried. But so far I've been able to stay just out of his reach. Lately it's become more and more difficult. He's a determined man, and my life is in his hands."

"I know," Trudl said, hanging her head even lower until Leisel couldn't see her face. "He's a hard man to stay away from."

A long-standing suspicion swelled in Leisel's chest. "Have you been able to . . . stay away from him, Trudl?" she asked.

Trudl batted her red lids as tears spilled down onto her cheeks. "I tried. Really, I did. But it didn't help. He . . . he did it, anyway."

Rage swept through Leisel, hot and searing. It was the color red. So the high and righteous Baron Schmidt was fornicating with his own daughter. Yet he had the power to put innocent people like Leisel's mother to death for their supposed sins.

At the sound of Trudl's quiet weeping, Leisel pushed her own anger aside and took her friend in her arms. "I'm sorry, Trudl," she said, folding her close. "I'm so sorry."

Leisel didn't know what else to do. What else to say. But it felt right simply to hold Trudl and whisper soothing words, so she did it. Her mother had told her that healing came naturally. But Leisel knew that it was much easier to heal a headache than to touch a heart that was aching, a heart that had been violated, like Trudl's.

Someday Baron Schmidt would pay for the pain he had inflicted. And Leisel swore, as she held her sobbing friend, that she would be there to see it.

Usually a walk in the moonlit forest brought a quiet solitude that dispelled Leisel's worries, but tonight nothing could calm her. That tight, aching feeling inside wouldn't go away. The moist night air couldn't cool her anger or take away her bitter need for revenge against the man who had hurt everyone she had ever loved.

The forest was silent; even the foxes and hares in the

bushes seemed to have deserted her tonight. Leisel moved through the darkness that was broken only by occasional shafts of silver light streaming through the trees. The pungent smell of decaying leaves, combined with the fresh scent of living things, filled her lungs as she breathed deeply. She had walked farther into the forest than usual, seeking answers to problems that seemed to have no solutions.

Then it came to her—softly on the damp night air. It was the song. The moon's song. His song.

Just as the moonlight shone in silver streams into the darkness, the high, clear tones cut through the silence. This was a different melody than before, but it went straight to her heart, giving her the peace she sought.

Unable to resist, she followed the sound. It was as though the music reached out to her, wrapped itself around her like a silver cord, and pulled her to its source, to him.

She found him in a meadow, sitting beside a small fire. As she stepped out of the trees into the moonlight, he stopped playing and turned to face her. He smiled, his eyes gleaming with satisfaction. He didn't seem surprised to see her here in the deepest part of the forest in the middle of the night.

He beckoned to her. "My lady, I'm so pleased you're here. Come and share my fire with me."

"I heard your music," she said as she sat down beside him and stretched her hands out to the warmth of the blaze. "It was so lovely, I had to follow it."

He smiled again, and she caught her breath at the beauty of his face. No mortal could be so handsome. He had to be the devil . . . or perhaps an angel.

"I must play more often," he said, laying the flute on a blanket beside him, "if this is what the pipe brings to me."

Leisel felt her face grow hot beneath his scrutiny. He was speaking to her as a man would speak to a woman he was courting. Feeling awkward and confused, she said nothing, but stared intently into the flames.

"Did you go walking in the forest tonight, hoping to lose your problems along the way?" he asked.

"Yes. I did. How did you know?"

He shrugged. "That's why I'm here tonight as well. I thought it might be the same for you."

Her eyes skimmed over his broad shoulders, his strong, capable arms and hands, and down to the heavy thigh muscles clearly outlined beneath his hose. She felt the power radiating from him and wondered what possibly could be troubling him. "What problems do you have? If I were you, I wouldn't worry about anything."

The moment the words were out of her mouth, she realized how childish they sounded and was embarrassed. But he seemed to understand.

"Your concerns are my concerns, my lady. I'm here to serve you. Surely you know that."

She blushed again and felt her throat closing. He couldn't mean it. He was only flirting with her, teasing her, yet he seemed sincere.

"You arrived just at the right moment this morning," she said. "The villagers were all ready to blame me for the rats."

"I know. You live in a town full of fools."

It was the first time Leisel had ever heard her own thoughts spoken aloud, and she was startled to feel the strength his words imparted.

"Why did you ask the baron to close the mine?" she asked. "He would have gladly paid you a small fortune in gold."

"I have enough gold."

She smiled. "No one has enough gold. Not even kings."

He chuckled and nodded. "That's true, I suppose. But despite its glow, gold cannot warm the heart. Besides, the children need my help, and so do you, my lady."

She studied him for a long time, the strong set of his jaw, the gleam of passion in his eyes, his proud, aristocratic posture. If she or the children had ever wished for a champion, surely this man was equal to the challenge.

"But why would you help me when you've only just met me?"

"I've known you forever."

His words grabbed at her heart and held it just as his song had. He spoke the truth—or at least it felt like the truth, even though she couldn't explain why.

She had seen this man before. She had heard his music and his voice. She had kissed him, touched him, and . . .

Turning her face away from him, she tried to push the thoughts to the back of her mind. But every time he moved, she was acutely aware of his body. She felt herself reaching out with her heart to touch him, to embrace him as though he were a lover who had been lost to her years and years ago. In another place, another time. Another life.

A dark, suffocating fear welled up inside her, the fear that she might lose him again. The faces of the men on the town council sprang into her mind, and her heart tightened in her chest.

"Can you really rid Hamelin of its rats?" she asked.

"What do you think?"

"I think you could do anything."

He turned and took her hands in his. It was the first time he had touched her, yet his hands felt so familiar, warm and strong, as they tightened around hers. "I can lure the rats out of the village," he said. "Don't worry. After all, I lured you here, didn't I?"

It was true. She had come because he had willed her to, because he had drawn her to him with his music.

"Watch," he said as he released her hand and picked up his flute. He lifted the pipe to his lips.

He played, his song filling the night air. As it had before, the melody wrapped itself around her in a silken cocoon that soothed her troubled spirit.

She stared into the fire, seeing beyond the flames to a

place deep inside her own heart. A land that was free of hatred and ignorance, with high mountains, towering trees, dark rivers, and vineyards that filled the air with the sweet scent of grapes. There was a castle there, a fortress with walls that were thick and strong, where she could feel safe and protected.

Leisel wanted to stay in that enchanting place forever, to explore the castle, to taste the wine of those vineyards, to live there day after day without fear. But the piper's song ended abruptly and the pastoral panorama faded from her mind's eye. Once again she was sitting beside the fire with the darkness tight around them.

But the black forest had changed. Just outside the golden ring of light cast by the fire, she saw shadows moving and the glow of eyes—animals' eyes. Startled, she looked around and saw that they were surrounded by forest creatures: deer, foxes, hares, squirrels, and other animal shapes that she couldn't discern.

"Don't be afraid," he said. "They won't hurt us."

She was afraid, but not of the animals. She was afraid of the power in this man—a power she'd recognized and tried to discount, a force that was undeniable.

Worse yet, she was fairly sure that he was here because she had summoned him, because she had asked the moon to send her help. By doing that, had she opened herself up to the powers of darkness, as Father Beck had so often warned them about? Had she unwittingly invited a demon—or even Satan himself—into her world?

"Who are you?" she asked. "What kind of man are you that you can summon the animals of the woods and they come to you like lapdogs?"

"I'm a man," he said with a shrug. "Like any other."

She shook her head. "I don't think so." Swallowing hard, she added, "Are you the devil?"

He said nothing for a long moment as he looked into her

eyes. Then he said, "There are some who say you're the devil's daughter. Are you my daughter, Leisel?"

"No." His question made her own assumption seem foolish.

"Then you have your answer." He reached out and softly stroked her cheek with his fingertips. The simple gesture went through her like a liquid that was hot and cold at the same moment.

"I'm not evil," he said, "and you have nothing to fear from me. Listen to your heart, Leisel. It will never lie to you. And neither will I."

How did he know those words, the words that her mother had said to her so many times? He and her mother emanated the same kind of power and spoke with the same wisdom. She remembered how the piper had healed Monika, and the similarities between him and her mother became frighteningly apparent. Recalling her mother standing before the town council, Leisel shuddered.

"Be careful," she said, reaching out to place her hand on his arm. It seemed such a natural thing to do, touching him. "They'll kill you if they can. If you get rid of the rats, they'll condemn you for witchcraft. Baron Schmidt will see you dead before he'll close down the mine."

"Don't worry, Leisel. All will go as it should tomorrow. Only believe." He squeezed her hand before releasing it. "But now you should go. I must prepare for the dawn. It will be here before long."

She rose, reluctant to leave him.

"Only believe," he said before she turned and walked away.

He watched until she disappeared into the trees, his face a mixture of sadness and affection. From the corner of his eye he saw a movement, a larger shape moving among the shadows. It was the silver wolf.

He smiled, lifted his pipe to his lips, and played. The circle of glowing eyes moved closer to the fire—except for the silver wolf, which followed Leisel into the darkness of the forest.

Seven

IT BEGAN AS a small scratching sound in the rafters of the stable, then grew louder and louder until the noise reverberated throughout the building.

"Leisel, what is that?" Monika asked, her voice heavy with sleep.

Leisel, who had just woke as well, was unable to identify the strange noise immediately. Then the grain in the horses' troughs began to stir. One by one tiny gray, black, and brown heads popped out and looked around. Whiskers twitched, and a high-pitched squeaking was added to the rustling.

"It's the rats," Leisel exclaimed as she quickly sat up and took the trembling Monika in her arms.

"What are they doing? What's wrong?" Monika asked, burying her face against her older friend's shoulder.

Slowly a knowing smile spread across Leisel's face, deepening the dimples in her cheeks and adding a twinkle to her green eyes. "Nothing's wrong. Nothing at all."

The exodus was an awesome sight. More than fifty rats of different sizes wriggled out of the straw and headed for the various cracks in the walls. Scores more scrambled down from the rafters, over the feed troughs and bales of hay. The stable was alive with them one minute, then, as quickly as it had begun, it was over. They were gone, and the barn was curiously silent and still.

"Where did they go?" Monika asked with relief.

"Come on, let's find out," Leisel said, jumping up from the straw and pulling on her slippers.

"Oh, no." Monika huddled into a ball and covered herself with her blanket. "If they're finally gone, I'm not going to go chasing them."

"Then go to sleep, *liebchen*," Leisel said as she tucked the blanket around the girl's chin. "I won't be gone long."

She ran out of the stable and into the pale morning light. The sun was just beginning to rise, and its feeble glow illuminated the strangest scene Leisel had ever witnessed.

Rats, thousands of them, poured from the houses, the outbuildings, and the fields into the craggy dirt road that led toward the center of town. The cacophony of squeaks was deafening, drowning out even the shouts of the excited citizenry, who were leaving their cottages to watch the unusual parade.

"What's happening?" someone shouted.

"It's the piper! The rats are following him!"

"He's leading them out of the village!"

Leisel could see him on the road ahead, his pipe to his lips, walking through the town, leading his army of rodents. The morning sun shone brightly on his golden hair and lit the dazzling colors of his cloak. He moved with the purposeful, regal stride of a king.

Leisel watched and felt the swell of pride in her chest. He was doing it! She hadn't been wrong to believe in him, after all. He had said that he would do it, and there, before the wide eyes of the stunned villagers, he was eliminating every trace of the furry, disease-ridden pests that had tormented them for months.

"Where is he leading them?" Leisel heard Rolf Gunter ask.

"It doesn't matter," shouted his wife as she grasped his arm and danced about with joy, "as long as it's far away from here."

"He's leading them toward the river," old Helga said as the piper turned at the fork in the road and headed down to the River Weser's banks. Leisel lifted her skirts and ran as fast as she could, keeping to the side of the road and away from the stream of fuzzy bodies that scrambled toward the water's edge.

By the time she reached the bank, she was out of breath but still amazed at the spectacle. She clutched the limb of an old oak tree that jutted out over the water and watched as he stepped into the river. He waded into the current until the water was near the tops of his thigh-high boots. Stopping there, he continued to pipe his merry tune, a march that lent a lively step to the eery parade.

Without hesitation the rats followed him: fat, lazy rats; thin, scruffy ones; tiny babies barely able to walk; and their graying grandparents; all spilling into the water, where they were swept downstream. The townspeople ran down to the riverbank, shouting with joy as the creatures that had made their lives miserable dived into the water and disappeared in the swirling dark torrent.

Caught up in the moment, Leisel found herself cheering along with the multitude. For once she was one with her community, captivated by the piper's magic.

Finally the stream of rodents slowed to a trickle. And less than an hour after it had all started, the last rat dived into the water, following his predecessors to a watery death.

Amid the crowd's cries of joy, the piper waded to the riverbank. His long cloak hung heavy with water as he bowed to his audience. Then he turned to Leisel and bowed to her alone. His gaze locked with hers, and in that moment Leisel forgot the watchful, hungry eyes of the crowd. Overcome with wonder at what she had just witnessed, she marveled that this remarkable man was the same one who had sat beside the fire with her only last night, the one who had told her he wanted to help her, the man who had said he had known her forever.

And Leisel knew as she stood there on the banks of the River Weser, returning his smile, that she would love him until the day she died.

The next day, as Leisel stood in the corner of the council hall and watched the scene before her, she couldn't help thinking how the mood of the villagers had changed in a matter of days. Two days ago they had been at one another's throats, attacking the council over the problem of the rats. Today they were a jubilant lot, boisterously celebrating their deliverance.

Only the council seemed subdued, the baron and Father Beck in particular.

The piper stood in front of them as he had before, tall and proud, radiating an authority that intimidated even the auspicious noblemen of Hamelin.

"Why has this council summoned me here?" the piper asked, his blue eyes piercing the baron's as he stared down at the corpulent mayor, seated behind the council table. "I thought our agreement was clear. I've fulfilled my part of the bargain. All that remains is for you to fulfill yours."

"Yes, well . . ." The baron paused and looked around the room at his happy constituency. "We've reconsidered. Your request is totally unreasonable. After a long night of soul-searching we've decided that it would be detrimental to the good people of Hamelin if Koppelberg Mountain were to be closed. This village depends upon the revenue from that mine, you see. So it is all-important to this community that it continue to function."

The piper's eyes narrowed, and his hand went to the hilt of his sword. "You made a bargain, Baron Schmidt. You gave your word as a nobleman. Are you saying now that you lied?"

The baron's face flushed, rivaling the red hues of his woolen robe. "I did not lie, sir. But after much thought, I feel that it is my duty to guard the best interests of this community."

"Are you certain it's the village's interests you guard, Baron, or your own?"

"I care only what is best for Hamelin. Here, this is the proof." He lifted a heavy bag of coins from inside his robe and set it down on the table in front of the piper. "This is from my own coffers," he said. "There are a thousand guilders here—more than enough to adequately compensate you for your trouble. And after all, it was our own good River Weser that killed the rats—and not you. Take your money and consider yourself fortunate to be paid at all."

Without a word the piper lifted the bag. He held it in his hand only a moment before ripping away its drawstring and flinging its contents onto the table before him. The room was silent but for the clinking of a few gold pieces as they hit the floor.

"How can you think that gold can buy what I did for this town?" he said. "If money could have rid you of your rats, your village would have been free of the pestilence long ago. Do you think gold can buy the lives of the children who work in that mine?"

No one spoke while the villagers looked at one another as though searching for the answer. The council members said nothing but stared straight ahead, pretending they couldn't see the man who stood before them.

"You made a bargain, sir," the piper said, lowering his voice to an ominously deep tone as he leaned across the table toward the baron. "And I warn you that justice is swift for swindlers and cheats. If you don't honor your agreement, you'll pay a grievous price."

"Are you threatening the good mayor's life?" Father Beck

asked, his gaunt face drawn in an unpleasant grimace. "Are you implying that you will work the same evil magic on him that you performed on the rats?"

"I simply speak the truth."

The piper turned his back to the council and faced the townspeople. His pale blue eyes scanned the crowd, searching each face in turn. "And what of the rest of you? Will you stand here and allow your mayor to renege on his promise?"

For a long moment no one spoke. Then old Helga shuffled forward on time-stiffened limbs. "I think the mine should have been closed long ago," she said. Her voice, which usually quivered, was strong and loud. "The baron made a promise to this man. Let's see to it that he keeps it."

Baron Schmidt and Father Beck glared at the old woman, but she didn't flinch as she surveyed the room with a challenging eye.

The piper smiled warmly down at her and placed one hand on her bony shoulder. "Is there another among you who has the courage to stand with this woman?"

No one moved. Rolf Gunter suddenly developed an acute interest in the tips of his slippers. Klaus, the miller, cleared his throat and crossed his arms defensively across his chest. The members of the council sat with stony faces that registered neither guilt nor even mild interest.

"Then you'll pay the price," the piper said. He glanced over at Leisel, and his eyes softened with compassion and sadness. "And perhaps it's a payment that's long overdue," he added as he turned and left the room.

After she'd finished serving the Schmidts' evening meal, Leisel went out looking for Trudl. The girl had seemed deeply troubled, hardly eating her food, on the verge of tears the entire time. Then she had abruptly excused herself from the table and run out the back door.

Neither the baron nor Eva had seemed to notice or care.

The baron had been sullen all day, mumbling under his breath about that "cursed piper." And his wife had remained silent and unobtrusive, for fear that he would direct his wrath toward her.

Leisel had searched the house, the stable, and the gardens for Trudl before finding her. She was sitting beside the pond that fed the baron's mill, his second most profitable enterprise after the mine. The girl was silently weeping into her apron.

Leisel sat down beside her and put her arm around her thin shoulders. "What's wrong, Trudl?" she asked. "Please tell me."

"I can't," she sobbed. "I can't tell anyone."

"But I'm your friend. Whatever it is, it can't be that bad."

Her sobs came harder and faster. "It *is* that bad. It's terrible."

Leisel pulled Trudl's apron away from her face and forced her to look at her. "So what is it?"

"I . . . I think I'm—" Her voice broke and she began to shake violently.

Leisel tightened her grip around her shoulders. "You're what?"

"I'm with child."

Leisel realized that she should have been shocked, but she wasn't. Only furious at the injustice of Trudl's dilemma.

"Who's the father?" she asked, although she knew. Trudl was a painfully shy girl. She never would have lain willingly with any of the village boys, even if they had been agreeable.

"I can't say." Trudl hung her head, and the shame on her face went straight to Leisel's heart. "I can never tell anyone."

"It doesn't matter. I know."

"You do?" Trudl looked startled, and Leisel wondered how she could have thought her secret safe.

"Of course I do. It was your own father who did this to you, wasn't it?"

Trudl nodded.

Neither woman spoke for a long time as Leisel held her friend and tried to impart some comfort, realizing that no amount of solace could change what had happened. The damage had already been done--to Trudl's body and to her heart.

Trudl's life was over before it had begun. The villagers would turn their backs on her. No "decent" person would ever again speak to her or even look her way. She would be branded for the rest of her life as a wicked woman and her child as a bastard. Even the fact that she was the baron's daughter wouldn't save her.

Leisel had seen this sort of thing before in Hamelin, and she had felt deeply for the young women. She knew, better than anyone, how it felt to be excluded from those around you, accused of wickedness.

Trudl sniffed and wiped her eyes on her apron. "Do you suppose the rats suffered a great deal? When they drowned, I mean," she said, staring out across the pond with a faraway look in her eyes.

Something in her tone chilled Leisel's heart. Desperate people sometimes committed desperate acts. And Leisel could sense the depth of her friend's despair as she sat beside her, holding her cold, trembling hand in hers, and trying to impart some comfort, some hope.

"Don't even consider that," Leisel said sternly, her hand tight on her friend's forearm.

"There's no other way."

"There's *always* another way."

"What?" Trudl looked at her, her swollen, lashless eyes wide with fear. "Tell me, what other way is there? I can't have this child, Leisel. I can't have my father's baby."

"I know. I know. Please don't cry, Trudl. I'll think of something."

The moment the thought entered her mind, Leisel wanted

to shut it out, but it was too late. She had remembered a way to help her friend, and there was no way to forget.

"There may be a way," she said carefully. "But you must never, never tell anyone. Only the two of us must ever know."

Trudl stopped crying and looked up at Leisel, a bit of hope in her swollen eyes. "What? What can I do?"

"There may be something that I can give you, some herbs that would cause the child to pass from your body now. It could make you ill, but—"

"It doesn't matter. Better sick than dead, and I swear, Leisel, I'll kill myself before I'll bring my own father's child into the world."

"I understand." And she did. She would rather die herself than to give birth to Baron Schmidt's son or daughter.

"How do you know about such an herb?" Trudl asked. "How do you know it will work?"

Leisel didn't know for sure. But she thought she remembered her mother speaking about such a potion. If such an herbal mixture existed, it would undoubtedly be recorded in her mother's spell book—the book she had sworn she would never open, let alone read.

"It doesn't matter how I know," she said, unable to trust even her closest friend with such damning knowledge. "And we won't know for certain if it works until we try."

Leisel's hands shook as she turned the pages made of thin goatskin. The golden light from her lantern lit the words that her mother had written in her neat, practiced hand.

Leisel had always taken pride in the fact that her mother could read and write. When Leisel was only five years old, her mother had begun to teach her how to form words on paper, telling her it was every mother's responsibility to pass these skills onto her children. In that way the art would be preserved from one generation to the next.

Leisel was proud of her ability to read, even though she had been warned not to reveal her skill to anyone in the village. Many times her mother had stressed the importance of keeping it a secret.

No other women in Hamelin could write, not even the baron's wife. But Leisel's mother hadn't been born in Hamelin. Leisel didn't know exactly where Katrina Kistner had come from, because she had died before Leisel had been old enough to ask the important questions.

Leisel knew only what the townspeople had told her: that her mother had arrived in Hamelin one morning, a babe in her arms, her long black hair tied back with a red silk scarf, wearing clothes that were too colorful, too daring. Despite the suspicions and curiosities of the townsfolk, Katrina had ignored their questioning gazes. Over the years she never revealed why she had a child but no husband, or where she was from, or why she was in Hamelin.

She had moved into a small cottage on the edge of town near the forest and began selling herbs to cure all sorts of ills. Immediately Father Beck had denounced her as a fraud and, worse yet, a witch. But her potions worked, and despite the priest's warnings, people had flocked to her door—often in the darkest part of the night—to seek remedies for everything from stomach upsets to male impotency.

Soon she had gained a reputation as an excellent midwife. Although the priest accused her of murdering the occasional stillborn and using its body for the devil's rituals, the citizens of Hamelin trusted Katrina Kistner with the lives of their mothers and newborns.

But eventually the poisoned stories began to spread and take root, and even those who owed their lives to the beautiful young healer began to doubt. Doubts became accusations, and accusations turned into blind hatred.

Leisel could feel her mother's healing power here on the pages of this book. It was more a diary than a book of spells, with each day's work meticulously entered for later reference.

Halfway through the book Leisel found the entry she had been looking for. A woman had come to Katrina Kistner, seeking a solution to her problem. She was young and betrothed to a older, wealthy man, a man she didn't love and didn't want to marry. But she was pregnant by the boy she did love. The man she was to marry was very jealous and powerful. If her love affair was discovered, both she and the boy would be killed.

The journal also revealed the name of the young woman. It was Eva Schmidt, Trudl's mother.

Below the entry were the instructions on how to prepare the potion that would cause the miscarriage.

Carefully Leisel studied the ingredients and directions. They were quite straightforward, a simple recipe. She already had most of the herbs hidden in the loft of the stable behind some loose boards.

But there was one powder she didn't have, sulfur. She knew what it was. The traders who came through sometimes had it, and she had seen the town physician using a bit of it in his poultices. It was yellow and smelled dreadful when dampened.

And she remembered when she had last seen it. The piper had used the yellow powder when he had prepared the wrap for Monika's arm. He had pulled a small pouch of it out of his bundle.

If she could only find him, Leisel was sure that he would give her a bit of the precious powder. She would search the forest for him; her instincts told her she would find him there in that wooded sanctuary. The thought of seeing him again thrilled her. Her pulse quickened at the prospect of speaking to him, of looking into his blue eyes and knowing that, for some reason which she couldn't fathom, he seemed to care for her.

She recalled the smile of affection he had given her that

morning as he stood on the riverbank. Yes, he would give her the powder if she asked him for it. In that moment Leisel realized with a sense of wonderment that the piper would deny her nothing.

She found him in the meadow again. Or rather, she found his fire, his haversack, and his blanket. She called for him, her voice echoing at the edge of the clearing. When there was no response, she stirred the embers of the fire, adding a bit of wood to it. Then she sat down and waited. Her heart pounded as her thoughts churned. Was she doing the right thing, giving this potion to Trudl? Was it a mortal sin to cause the death of a child who was not yet ready to come into the world? Doubt gnawed at her, and she ached in the deepest part of her spirit.

She felt a peace when she bound an injured limb or mixed a potion to dispel a fever. But this . . . was this healing or harming?

Around and around her mind swirled. Was it right to destroy the child to save Trudl's life? She was certain that if she didn't help Trudl, the girl would take her own life. Either way there was death. Trudl's way would mean two deaths.

It was her only recourse. Not the good choice, because there was no good choice to be made. But she would do it, she decided, sitting there beside the piper's fire, and she would live with her doubts.

She waited for what seemed to her a long time, but still he didn't appear. Thoughts of Trudl made her nervous and restless. What if she grew impatient or discouraged, thinking that Leisel had deserted her? Leisel thought of the rats, floundering in the torrent, and fear welled up inside her. She needed that powder now, and it was there in his bundle. Surely he would understand if he knew the circumstances.

Carefully she lifted the makeshift satchel onto her lap and untied it. She felt like a thief, yet she couldn't deny her curiosity and excitement at the privilege of glimpsing his most personal possessions.

She didn't find the small pouch containing his herbs. Instead she found objects that only heightened her wonder: a small wand made of oak with thin silver, copper and gold threads twisted decoratively around it. A stone was affixed at one end of the rod; it was a faceted gem with a pointed tip. The wand seemed to vibrate with the same kind of power she sensed when she touched her mother's book.

Gently she laid the rod aside and reached in again. This time she withdrew a silver cup. She had never known anyone who owned such a treasure. The only silver goblet she had ever seen had been in the church and was used for communion. Even the baron's cup was made of hammered pewter.

Next she pulled out a bag of coins, strange coins that she had never seen before. Holding one up to the light, she tried to read the inscription, but the language was unfamiliar to her. Peering at the face on the coin, she gasped. The surface was embossed with a rendering of the piper's face; she would have recognized his distinctive profile anywhere.

Why was his face on a coin? Only kings had their faces on—

A sound behind her made her jump. She sprang to her feet, dropping the bag of coins onto the ground. The piper stood there at the edge of the brambles, watching her with eyes that pricked her sensitive conscience.

"So I'm to be robbed, it seems. And by such a comely highwayman. You've stolen my heart already. Do you want my gold, as well?"

She blushed and stared down at the spilled coins that glittered in the firelight. "I would never steal from you, my lord. I meant only to take a bit of your yellow powder for a friend of mine who is . . . sick. I would have waited until you returned, but I'm afraid that she is in a desperate state, and time is of the essence."

"Your concern for your friend is admirable," he said as he sat down beside the fire. He reached up and pulled her down beside him. "But your friend will wait until you return. She knows you will help her. She trusts you."

Her eyes searched his, wondering how much he knew. It didn't matter, she decided. If this man knew her secrets, they were safe in his keeping.

She began to pick up the coins, trying to ignore the face so clearly imprinted on each one. But she couldn't resist asking the questions that were burning in her mind.

"Who are you?" she asked, her voice soft and breathy. "Who are you that you would have your face on gold coins? Only a king is honored in such a way . . . or the pope." She smiled. "And I don't think you're the pope."

He threw back his head and laughed a hearty, lusty laugh. "No," he said, "I'm not the pope." Then he sobered. "So I must be a king."

Leisel shuddered. She was sitting here beside a monarch. She could reach out and touch this man who was a king. With all her heart she *wanted* to reach out and touch him, knowing all the while that no one was allowed to think such thoughts about a king.

"Where are you from?" she asked, hoping he would not be offended by her blunt inquiry.

In reply he pointed toward the southeast. "From there. The Bohemian Mountains. The mountains in my country are much higher than your Koppelberg. The land is rich with sweet vineyards, and my castle is a strong fortress." A look of incredible sadness crossed his face. "But not strong enough," he added. "My walls were thick and high enough to withstand the attacks of many armies. But they did nothing to protect my people from the illness that swept through my kingdom last winter."

Leisel laid her hand on his broad shoulder and felt his pain. "Did many of them die?"

"Many. Especially the children. My city was a quiet and lonely place this spring without the sound of the children's laughter in the streets."

His hand went to his sword and gripped the jeweled hilt in an unconscious gesture. "Here in this village they have children, so many of them. Yet they misuse them in that cursed mine. Something must be done. I won't leave here until those children are set free."

"Is that why you came to Hamelin?" she asked.

He smiled, his eyes tracing every feature of her face. "It was one reason." He reached into the haversack and pulled out a tiny crown set with pearls.

Leisel caught her breath. She had never seen anything so beautiful, so delicate. It had obviously been crafted for a woman.

He caressed it for a moment, then carefully returned it to his bundle. "I came for the children," he said, "but I came for myself, as well."

As she looked up at him, Leisel felt a feeling grow inside her that she had never felt before. She wanted so much to hold out her arms to him and have him fold her to his broad chest, to feel him embrace her and hold her close, to absorb some of his strength.

To feel protected and safe, even for a moment, would be heavenly. There seemed so much to be afraid of these days.

"Please, be careful," she said. "Baron Schmidt and Father Beck are formidable enemies. The townspeople are grateful for what you did, but they won't stand up for you. They'll watch you die, just like they watched my—"

He placed his hand on hers and squeezed. "I know. Don't worry about me. How about yourself? Aren't you afraid of what they may do to you?"

She shrugged. "Being afraid won't change what they do. If they decide to rob me of my tomorrows, I may not be able to stop them. But I'll not allow them to destroy today by making me afraid."

Admiration lit his eyes as he studied her. "Where did you learn such wisdom?" he asked.

"From my mother."

"She must have been a wonderful woman."

"She was."

"But the villagers . . . robbed her of her tomorrows?"

"They accused her of being the devil's mistress, of flying through the air on a pole dipped in a baby's blood, and of changing herself into a wolf. Then they killed her."

"I'm sorry."

Before she knew what he was doing, he placed his hand behind her head and drew her to him. With incredible gentleness he pressed his lips to hers. For a blissful moment she felt the soft firmness of his lips, the moist warmth of his breath. Then he pulled away.

"They won't kill you, my lady," he whispered. "I won't allow it."

Then, as quickly as he had pulled her to him, he turned, reached into his bundle, and pulled out the small leather pouch. "Here," he said, pressing it into her palm. "Take this to your friend. She needs you now."

Leisel hesitated a moment, loath to leave him. But her duty to Trudl was clear, so she stood and hurried down the path as quickly as her shaking legs would take her. She had only gone a little way into the forest when she stopped for a moment and leaned against a tree for support.

She thought of the coins that bore his image. She thought of the children who had died in his village. She thought of the tiny crown with the pearls. But mostly she thought of the way his lips had felt against hers. She could still feel and taste his kiss.

Then, with a tremendous effort, she shoved all those thoughts deeper into her heart where they would stay until she had a chance to take them out again. With a newfound determination she hurried back to Trudl.

Eight

SOMETHING WAS WRONG. Leisel knew it about three hours after she had given Trudl the potion. The pain had started almost immediately and had increased until Trudl was writhing on her bed with her arms clutched around her abdomen.

Leisel warned her that there would be some discomfort; her mother's journal had mentioned that a certain amount of pain was to be expected. But neither of them had anticipated this unbearable agony.

And there was so much blood. Leisel couldn't understand how such a small person could lose so much and still be alive.

"Leisel, help me," she gasped between sobs. "It hurts so much. I don't think I can stand it."

As she stood there by the bedside and watched her friend suffer, Leisel felt the same terrible sense of helplessness that she had felt when her mother died, and she had been forced to stand by and watch. She had been a child then. Now she was a woman, and there had to be something she could do.

There *was* something. Under any other circumstances she wouldn't even have considered it; it was simply too danger-ous. But she couldn't let Trudl die.

"I'll be right back," she said, leaning over her patient and wiping the perspiration from her forehead. "I promise I won't be long."

Leaving Trudl's room, she hurried as quietly as possible down the corridor to Eva Schmidt's bedchamber. After softly rapping three times on the door, she pushed it open. At first she was afraid she might find the baron inside. But then it occurred to her that Baron Schmidt probably had not visited his wife's bedchamber since nine months before Trudl's birth.

In the darkness she found the baroness lying on her bed, a cloth across her brow. A heavy drape was hung across the window to block out the light of the sun.

"Who is it?" the woman asked, pushing one of the bed curtains aside. "Oh, Leisel. What do you want?"

"It's Trudl. She's very sick, and I think you could help her."

"Trudl?" She sat up on the bed and took the cloth from her head. "What's wrong with her?"

"Womanly problems," Leisel said, not meeting her eyes. "Please come quickly." She turned and rushed from the bedroom. Eva followed closely behind, pulling on a robe as she scurried down the hall.

They entered Trudl's room, and Leisel was instantly aware of the thick, cloying smell of blood. When Eva saw the crimson-stained cloths and her daughter curled into a tight ball of pain, she gasped and rushed to the girl's side.

"Mother, no," Trudl said. "Leisel, you shouldn't have told her."

"I had to." Leisel took the Trudl's hand. "Don't worry. She can help us. Can't you?" Leisel looked across the bed at the baroness, whose face was as white as her daughter's.

"What's happening here?" she asked. "What have you girls done?"

"The same thing that you and my mother did years ago," Leisel said carefully. "I tried to help Trudl, just the way my mother helped you. But something's wrong. You've gone through this yourself. I was hoping perhaps you might remember something that would help."

Dazed, Eva stared at Leisel. At first she shook her head as though to deny her words. But as she looked down at her daughter she bit her lip, fighting back the tears that filled her eyes. Sitting on the edge of the bed, she took her child in her arms.

"There, there, my love. I know how much it hurts. But it'll pass soon and the pains will stop."

Turning to Leisel, she said, "How long ago did you give her the herbs?"

"About four hours now."

"Then this is the worst time. I'll tell you what your mother did for me, and we can do it now for Trudl. Take a clean sheet from the chest over there and tear it into strips. We'll use them as packing to slow the bleeding. And we can give her some of the elixir that the physician gives me for my headaches. That will help to ease her pain."

Leisel quickly did her bidding, while Eva held her daughter and gently rocked her.

"Mother," Trudl said when the elixir was finally beginning to relieve some of her pain, "I'm so sorry."

Eva stroked Trudl's cheek and brushed the strings of sweat-dampened hair back from her face. Then Eva looked across the bed at Leisel. "I know, my darling," she said. "I know. We're all sorry."

Hours later the bleeding had stopped and Trudl slept comfortably. Her face was ashen but relaxed, with no trace of residual pain. Leisel and Eva sat on the foot of the bed and watched the steady rise and fall of her breathing. For the first time since the ordeal had begun, Leisel felt that all would be well with her friend.

Eva Schmidt's face, however, wasn't as peaceful as her

daughter's. When Leisel noticed the sorrow in her eyes, she felt a stab of sympathy for her.

"He's a beast," Eva said, her voice hushed and bitter. "He should die for what he's done to this child. And to the other children."

Leisel said nothing but stared down at Eva's hands as they knotted and twisted in her lap. In all the years that Leisel had known Eva Schmidt, the lady had never confided in her, had never expressed an opinion on any matter. But the crisis they had faced together had broken down the wall between mistress and servant.

"He's going to open the mine again," the baroness continued. "Can you imagine? After the tragedy that happened before, he's going to risk it. He's going to send all of those children down into that hell again. It doesn't matter to him that he's robbing them of their health and childhood, not to mention risking their lives."

"After seeing what he's done to his own child," Leisel said, "I can't think that anyone matters to Baron Schmidt except himself."

"Did my husband know about . . . this?" She nodded toward Trudl and the pile of bloody cloths.

"No one knows, except the three of us."

"Then it must stay that way. If anyone discovered what happened here tonight, all three of our lives would be destroyed."

"I understand." Leisel was silent for several moments, then she said, "But as long as this is kept secret, your husband will remain unpunished for his crime against your daughter."

"Yes, I know. The thought makes me more angry than you can imagine. But my husband is a formidable foe. Long before we could bring him to justice, we would be ruined. That is, if we used normal means to destroy him . . ."

Leisel studied her carefully, but the baroness's eyes were guarded, wary. "What do you mean?"

"I mean that there are other ways. Your mother knew of such ways."

Leisel glanced over at Trudl, who continued to sleep peacefully. "My mother was killed for her knowledge of those things which are forbidden."

A look of pain and remorse crossed Eva's lined face, a face too old for its years. "I know. I'll always remember that horrible night. She was my friend, you know. But I stood there and watched her die. It was my husband's fault that she died. He lied about her and . . . but that's all over now. Nothing can bring her back. But you, Leisel, you're stronger than she was."

"Stronger? Than my mother?" Leisel was stunned. She had always idolized her mother. It had never occurred to her to compare herself or her power to her mother's.

"Yes. Your mother was a rare and wonderful woman. But so are you, Leisel. Look at what this town has done . . . what *we've* done to you. And yet you're strong—and generous. Only a special spirit could withstand that much punishment and go on loving."

The tears that had filled Eva's eyes now spilled down her cheeks and onto her lap. "I'm not that strong," she said. "And neither is my Trudl. *He* broke our spirits, a long time ago."

Leisel reached over and clasped Eva's hand. It was cold and limp in hers, as though the life was gone from it. "If he had broken you completely, you'd never have been able to help your daughter tonight. You're still capable of caring, still able to love."

Eva closed her eyes and a sob caught in her throat. "God curse that man," she said when she had found her breath. "Someone must stop him. He can't be allowed to send those children back into that mine. He mustn't have the chance to harm Trudl ever again."

Leisel thought of the piper. She thought of what Eva had

said about the "other ways" to deal with Baron Schmidt.

The baroness had said that she was stronger than her mother had been. Could that possibly be true? Did that mean that perhaps she could use her mother's magic against the baron and bring an end to the suffering?

Leisel patted the baroness's hand and said, "Don't cry. Maybe someone will."

Leisel sat on the bank of the River Weser and watched the dark waters flow by her feet. Not a trace of the rats remained, the river having accomplished its task and eliminated the plague forever. The rippling water sparkled in the moonlight, and the beauty of it brought a quiet peace to Leisel's spirit.

Three days had passed since Trudl's miscarriage, and slowly she was getting stronger. Looking back, Leisel wasn't sure if she had done the right thing. She had given her friend the potion out of love, and that was what mattered in the end. When she thought of Eva, who'd grown old before her time, and of Trudl, whose childhood had been cut short, Leisel couldn't help hating the man responsible. Eva was right. He had to be stopped, but how?

Her thoughts were interrupted by a sound carried to her on the night breeze, a happy sound. In an instant her heart recognized it. It was the piper, walking in her direction along the opposite bank of the river.

But it was the children who scampered behind him that brought a smile to Leisel's face. They were the children from the mine: little Hans, his gnomelike face lit with a smile; his brother, Sigmund, dancing as though his bandaged leg felt no pain. And the sight that Leisel welcomed most— Monika, skipping in the piper's wake, her auburn curls bouncing in the sunlight.

They bore no resemblance to the frail, motley group she had been nursing. Their movements were so blithe, Leisel barely recognized them as they squealed, jumped, sang, and whirled to the piper's music. For the first time in most of their lives the little paupers were like other children, care-free and joyful, dancing with total abandon.

In that moment she loved him, this man who could impart such happiness with his pipe, whose own joyful spirit was expressed in his music and passed on to others. His song lifted all who listened above the problems of this life into a world where there was no pain, no worry, no hatred. His music transported listeners to a land that glittered silver like the moon, a land they had always known in their hearts but had never visited.

Almost as soon as he had appeared, he and his entourage were gone, disappearing around the bend in the river. As she watched him go, Leisel felt an odd sense of loss. Although he had never even looked her way, she felt touched by him, by his music. In her body, mind, and spirit she felt stronger, rejuvenated.

Leisel closed her eyes and concentrated on that feeling of power deep inside her, gathering it together, feeling it, test-ing it.

She would need every kernel of strength she could muster for the fight ahead. It was a battle she couldn't afford to lose.

He had known that he would find her there, standing beside the hollow tree in the deepest part of the forest. He hadn't known that she would be crying. And he hadn't expected her to throw herself into his arms the moment he spoke her name.

"Leisel, what is it?" the piper said as he gathered her to his chest and stroked her long black hair. It was much softer than he had expected, and he was somehow surprised that it felt so natural to be holding her. "Tell me why you're cry-ing."

"Here," she said, reaching beneath her cloak and pulling

out a leather-bound journal. "It's my mother's book. She wrote in it daily, everything that happened to her. I've always wanted to read it, but I've only dared to glance at it from time to time. The council says such writing is evil and forbidden. I could be burned at the stake just for having this book."

He pulled her into a patch of moonlight and eased her down to the ground, where they settled on a thick bed of fragrant pine needles. When he sat beside her and reached for the book, she clasped it tightly to her breast.

"What does it say, Leisel?" he asked. "What did you read that made you cry?"

"I read what he did to her."

"Who?"

She gulped and swallowed her tears. "Baron Schmidt. He caused her death. If it weren't for his treachery, my mother would be alive today. He hurt her, and lied about her, and caused her to be convicted of witchcraft."

"Tell me about it. Tell me everything," he said. "I need to know it all."

She told him, and his anger turned to fury as he listened. She told him how Schmidt had pursued her mother, constantly trying to have his way with her. The young woman had denied him, knowing that she was placing her life in jeopardy by doing so.

One day, tired of waiting, the baron had forced himself on her. She had fought him, but he had raped her at knifepoint. In the struggle, her left hand had been severed.

Later that day, weak from the loss of blood, she had stumbled into the town hall and accused Schmidt before the council. He had denied the rape and mutilation, but told a story of how he had been hunting that morning in the forest and had been attacked by a large wolf. The baron claimed that he had defended himself against the beast and cut off its front left paw.

Father Beck had come to the baron's defense, saying that this was indeed proof that Katrina was a witch. That she was capable of "shape changing," an evil practice common to all servants of the devil.

By seeking justice, Katrina Kistner had unwittingly delivered herself into the hands of her enemies. The baron's lie provided the "evidence" they needed to condemn her to death. "The baron lied, the council believed him, and the villagers killed her," Leisel said as she ended her story.

They sat quietly for a long time, neither of them speaking as they thought about the young woman whose only sin had been that of healing others. Yet she had been raped, her body and spirit violated by the baron, and then by an entire village. Her death had been a one of the most painful known to man, and to what purpose, other than to satisfy the evil in Baron Schmidt?

Finally the piper spoke. "And now you want to kill the baron."

"Yes, I want to kill him. I want to avenge the deaths of those children who were lost in the mine, and I want to make sure that the survivors never have to return. I want justice for what he did to my mother. I can use her own magic, the magic in this book, to destroy him. Surely you don't think that's wrong."

He took her hands in his and looked directly into her eyes, pulling her into him. "I understand your anger," he said. "And I agree that he needs to pay for the misery he's caused. I also recognize the strength of your mother's magic and your ability to use it. You're a powerful woman. You must make the choice every day to use your power for good or evil, to act out of love or hatred."

"Are you saying I shouldn't fight him?"

"I don't care what happens to him. He's a wicked man who will come to an evil end—that much is already ordained. But I do care about you. And I know that you are a healer, not a killer. If you use your power out of hatred, it will poison your spirit, and you will be the one who is hurt in the end."

He reached out with one hand and brushed her hair back from her face. The silver streak glittered among the black, and he thought he had never seen such a beautiful sight as this woman's face in the moonlight. "I don't want to see you hurt again, my lady," he said. "You've suffered enough already."

With his palm cupping her chin, he forced her to look up at him. "Please tell me that you'll think about what I've said, that you'll be careful."

She nodded, but her eyes refused to meet his. He knew instinctively that she was going to do it and that there was nothing he could do to stop her. He only hoped he could protect her through the course of events that she was about to set into motion.

"Everyone in the village is saying that the baron is going to open the mountain again in four days. And he announced that all of us will have to go back into the mine," Monika said, her amber eyes round with fear. "You said I wouldn't have to go back, Leisel. You promised."

"I know I promised. Don't worry." Leisel covered the child with her ragged horsehair blanket and tucked it around her neck.

"But I'm scared, Leisel. I don't want to go down into the mine again. It's so dark in there that you can't see what's ahead of you in the tunnel. And it's so small, you can hardly move. I got stuck one time and was there for hours before Hans found me and pulled me out. I thought I was surely dead. And the air stinks so bad, like rotten eggs. You can hardly stand to breathe it."

"You won't have to go, little one. Truly. I'll find a way somehow. Just go to sleep now and try to have sweet dreams."

Sweet dreams, Leisel thought. Such an irony for a child who had never known a world without pain and suffering. Leisel patted the girl's shoulder, then walked over to stand beside the stable window. Tonight, even the silver moonlight did nothing to calm the turbulence inside her, the storm that had been brewing since she had read those words in Katrina's journal. Leisel hated the baron for what he had done to her mother. And somehow, she would find the means to destroy him.

"There's one way you can make sure the girl never goes into the mine again," said a voice behind her.

She whirled around and saw the baron standing there, a sardonic grin splitting his round face. He reached out to touch her and in an instinctive gesture she pushed his hand aside.

It was the first time she had ever openly defied him, and the moment wasn't lost on either of them.

"Don't you *ever* do that again, girl," he said as he grabbed her by the shoulders and shook her. His breath was sour on her face; she turned her head away. "If I want to touch you, I'll touch you and you'll allow it. Do you understand?"

She lifted her chin and glared up at him, answering him with the fire in her eyes. From his shocked expression she realized it wasn't the answer he had been expecting.

She was surprised when he moved away from her instead of pressing his advantage. So the baron wasn't accustomed to having someone stand her ground with him. She wondered if anyone had ever dared to defy him. Then she remembered her mother, the one woman who had. Red hatred flared inside her, and for once she didn't try to keep it from showing on her face.

"You'll regret this, Leisel," he said, his voice quivering with rage. "You're a peasant. I'm your master. You'd better not forget that." When she continued to glare at him, he turned abruptly on his heel and marched out of the stable, slamming the heavy door behind him.

Still battling to keep her fury in check, Leisel stared down at the tracks that his boots had made in the dust of the stable floor. She stood there for a long moment, making up her mind.

Then, her decision made, she walked over to the footprints and knelt beside them. Without hesitation she took off her apron and laid it on the ground. Slowly, carefully, she scooped up the dust from first one print, then another, and laid the dirt in the center of her apron.

Having done that, she dusted off her hands, gathered the apron into a bundle, and tied it with its strings, taking care that none of the dust spilled. After one last look at Monika, who had slept through her visit from the baron, Leisel tucked the apron under her arm and left the stable.

The moon had slipped behind the clouds. Here in the deepest part of the forest the only light came from the fire burning in the center of the small clearing. Beside the fire knelt Leisel, her beautiful face glowing from the heat of the blaze, her black hair glistening in the firelight. But the hatred that twisted her face marred its perfection.

On her lap lay an open leather book. In her hand was a white cloth tied into a bundle. After consulting the book she carefully untied the cloth, which contained a small pile of soil and dust.

Closing her eyes, she chanted some ancient, mystic words.

She repeated the litany three times, then opened her eyes and held the apron over the fire. The flames caught the cloth and immediately curled upward. She held the garment as long as she could. At the last moment, when the heat was too intense to bear, she dropped the apron into the fire.

Referring to the book once more, she reached into the full sleeve of her tunic and pulled out a leather pouch. With careful consideration she measured a small amount of a powder into her palm, then sprinkled the powder into the flames.

Once again she closed her eyes and began to chant. She prayed for several minutes, her voice becoming louder and louder until it filled the forest. It was a sound that was unfamiliar to the dense stand of trees, the mossy slopes of the hills, the berried brambles of the undergrowth. It was foreign because it was bitter and angry, because it disturbed the forest's natural tranquillity.

Then it happened. The fire exploded. Blue, green, and purple tongues of flame leaped upward, soaring higher than the woman's head as clouds of black, pungent smoke billowed out of the charred cloth. The inferno roared for several minutes; then, as quickly as it had begun, the flames died down to a pile of glowing embers.

It was only then that the young woman stopped her chanting. She was satisfied.

Nine

LONG BEFORE SHE reached the Schmidt estate, Leisel saw the glow of the fire that lit the night sky. From far away she heard the commotion, the shouts of the villagers as they tried to extinguish the blaze that was rapidly consuming the baron's mill.

Her heart pounding in her chest, Leisel stood on the riverbank and watched the frantic activity on the other side. Baron Schmidt's mill, second in his heart only to the mine, burned with a mighty vengeance. The lurid red flames sent showers of sparks shooting into the darkness, a spectacle that was reflected in the river at her feet.

Could she have caused it? she wondered as she breathed in the heavy smoke that floated her way on the wind. Her forest ritual had been so quick, so simple. Could it have caused this catastrophe?

She saw the baron running around like a Christmas goose who had just been robbed of his head, his arms flapping, his squawks louder than the roar of the fire and the shouts of the bucket-toting men. Apparently this was a great loss for him. Had her mother's magic, sifted through her hands, truly caused this?

Leisel hoped so.

On the other side of the river another young woman stood in the dark shadows, leaning weakly against a tree, watching. Her arms were wrapped tightly around her abdomen, as though she could control her pain by gripping it tightly. But she wore a smile, too. A self-satisfied smile. The smile of one who had finally won a battle in a lifelong war.

Two nights later, guided by her own troubled spirit, Leisel went into the woods in search of the piper. She found him sitting beside a campfire in the meadow. Somehow she hoped he would play his beautiful moon song to make her heart forget . . . Trudl's pain, the death of her friend's unborn child, and the destruction of the baron's mill. At the time the fire had seemed like a victory over the baron. But since that night Leisel had realized that the fiery destruction of the mill had hurt more than the baron's money coffers. The mill had helped to feed a village of people who were now suffering because of her actions.

As doubts and misgivings assailed her, she felt the need to be with the piper. Too much had happened since she had seen him last, and she wanted to feel the quiet peace and strength that seemed to flow from him.

He was sitting, quietly drinking from his silver cup. When he saw her, he smiled and beckoned her to sit beside him. "Would you join me in some mead?" he asked, extending his goblet to her.

She took the cup, and the darkness of her mood brightened a bit. It helped to be sharing the same cup with him, to see the joy in his eyes when he looked at her. She supposed the same pleasure was shining in hers as she gazed at his handsome face and his golden hair.

Tilting the cup, she sipped the warm, amber liquid and gasped as it traced a fiery trail to her belly. Within moments she felt a hot tingling spread through her limbs, into her fingertips and feet.

"It's very nice," she said, handing him back the cup. "I've never tasted anything like that before."

"There are many things you've never experienced before, my lady," he said, and something in the way his eyes swept over her made her heart beat a bit faster. "There are many pleasures in this world for a man and woman to discover together. You and I . . . we can find the joy in this moment, the discoveries to be made in this one night."

He reached out and touched her hair. The gesture went through her, liquid fire, like the mead.

"So lovely," he whispered. "I never dreamed you would be so lovely."

He turned and lifted something from his bundle. It was small and wrapped in a black scarf. Carefully he unwound the cloth and revealed a deck of cards. "Here," he said, fanning them out for her to see. "We'll look into the cards and see what tonight may hold."

The cards looked very old to Leisel, and they were strange, unlike any playing cards she had ever seen before. The pictures on them were intricately drawn portraits. They depicted kings and knights lifting jeweled swords that pierced the clouds above their heads, queens drinking from silver and gold cups, strange characters and scenes that revealed every joy and suffering of mankind.

"What are they?" she asked breathlessly, almost afraid of his answer. There was power in the cards, the same power that radiated from the man who held them in his hand.

"They're special cards," he said. "They can tell you what happened before, what's happening now, and what's yet to come."

Leisel drew back, shaking her head. "I don't think I want to know the future."

"Why not? If it's a bright future, you can look forward to it with eagerness. It might make the darkness of tonight a little easier to bear."

"But what if it's bad?"

"If the cards tell you that the future will be bad, they will also tell you how to change it to make it better."

She said nothing but simply watched as he shuffled the deck from one hand to the other.

"Would you like to see into the future, my lady?" he asked, his smile beguiling. Again it occurred to her that this man could be the devil, come to snatch away her soul. Perhaps the priest was right and the devil could appear to be beautiful, like an angel of light.

But then she thought of her mother's admonition to listen to her heart's voice. Her heart told her this man was good. His blue eyes looked directly into hers without wavering. She felt as if he could see into her heart, yet she felt no need to hide from him.

"Yes," she said, "let the cards show me my past and my future."

With his eyes closed, he held the cards against his chest for a moment, then took several deep breaths. She didn't know what he was doing, but somehow she recognized the gesture. It was all new and strange, yet old and familiar. Once again he shuffled the cards, then spread them like a fan, facedown on the ground before her. "Here," he said, "choose one that will show us your past."

She picked one and handed it to him. He turned it over, and her heart leapt into her throat. It was a picture of a woman who was bound to a stake. Her hair was blowing wildly in the wind, and swords were thrust into the ground forming an imprisoning circle around her.

"It's the card of a woman who longs to be free," he said. "A woman enslaved by the narrow-mindedness of those around her. They hold her captive with their ignorance and their hatred. She feels helpless to throw off the chains that are squeezing the life from her."

Leisel said nothing. She couldn't. Her heart was filling her throat and choking her. How could those cards have known how she felt?

"Do you long to be free, Leisel?" he asked, his voice soft and full of compassion.

She nodded and bit her lower lip to keep it from trembling.

"Then you shall be. Don't worry. Those chains will soon be gone. I promise you."

For a moment, looking into his eyes, she could almost believe it. Perhaps there was a chance that she would be free someday, free from the dark, oppressive feeling that was closing around her, blacker and tighter every day.

"Draw one for the future," he said.

Her hand trembled as she reached down again and chose yet another card. She handed it to him and closed her eyes, afraid to look.

"Don't be frightened," he said.

She dared to open her eyes. What she saw made her close them again. But even behind closed lids her mind's eye could see the gruesome picture. The Grim Reaper stood, scythe in hand, the ground at his feet littered with the corpses of the slain. She didn't need the piper to tell her that this card represented death—hers.

"It doesn't mean what you think," he said. "It's a good card to draw. Really. It means that your life, as you've lived it so far, will soon come to an end. But there is never an end without another beginning."

She opened her eyes and stared up at him, refusing to look down at the hideous card. "Am I going to die soon?" she asked.

In a movement that surprised her, he reached out and cupped her chin in his palm and lifted her face to his. Gently he kissed her, then caressed her cheek. His lips tasted like the mead and his hands were just as warm and intoxicating. "Do you think I would let them kill you?" he said. "I've looked for you all my life. I've no intention of losing you now."

His words confused her. How could he have been looking for her? This man was a king. Why would he put himself between her and harm?

"Choose another," he said. "Let's see your present."

Leisel reached for the third card, thinking that she didn't need a card to see her present. He *was* her present. This man with eyes that saw into her soul and a smile that told her he liked what he saw. This man who swore he would protect her, even when his cards said she would die.

In the present his face was all she could see. His mouth and the mead were all she could taste, and all she could feel was the warmth on her cheek where his fingers had caressed her.

She handed him the card and he turned it over. It was a picture of a man and a woman, both nude, standing in the midst of a beautiful garden. Their arms were wrapped around each other and they were looking deeply into each other's eyes. The woman had long black hair with a silver streak, and the man's hair was the color of sunlight. Leisel blinked her eyes. Could the mead be causing her to see visions?

Even as she watched, the figures seemed to move, the man's hands trailing down the woman's body, the woman welcoming his attentions by drawing him closer. Perhaps it was the flickering firelight. Perhaps it was her own imagination, her own desires coming to life there on the card.

Leisel stole a glance up at the piper and sensed that he was seeing the same vision. A heated blush spread over her face, a flush that had nothing to do with the mead or the fire. A warmth enveloped her, concentrating in the most intimate parts of her body. Leisel had never experienced that sensation before, and it frightened her.

"I'm scared," she whispered.

In a heartbeat he had gathered her into his arms, holding

her tightly against his chest. She could hear the beating of his heart and somehow she felt better just knowing that it was beating as fast and as hard as her own.

"Don't be afraid of anything you see in the cards, Leisel," he said. "Please, don't be afraid of me." His left hand stroked her hair while his right slid around her waist, pulling her even closer to him. "What do you want, my lady?" he said, pressing a kiss to her cheek. "Whatever you want of me, I'll do."

Leisel wasn't sure what she wanted. Desire was strong in her body, in her heart. But modesty prohibited her from speaking of her need. "Just let me stay with you forever," she said. "Like this, in your arms. I'm so tired of it all. I just want to rest. And I feel safe when I'm with you."

He laughed softly and eased her down onto the blanket spread beneath them. "Then rest, my love. Sleep and I'll keep your fears at bay. At least for a while."

Putting his arms around her, he pulled her to his side and wrapped the blanket over them both. She laid her head on his chest, snuggling into the comforting warmth of his body. In a moment she was asleep.

The cold gray mist of dawn fell on Leisel's face as she walked down the road toward Koppelberg Mountain. She had walked this wheel-rutted road more than a thousand times before, but her journey had always been the same— until now.

Her feet made no sound on the hard-packed dirt; her steps were those of a dreamer. She breathed in the clean scent of morning, filling her lungs with the cool, moist air. In the distance she could hear the piper's song, a happy melody, a march like the one he had been playing for the children when he had led them along the river's edge.

She came upon them when she rounded a bend in the road. The piper was leading, and the village children followed, dancing and singing. Pauper and craftsman's son, miner and the councilman's daughter, they skipped along behind him, heading toward the mountain.

She followed at the end of the line, caught up in the joy of the moment. His music was like golden sunshine, cutting through the gloom of the morning fog, lifting her into a place of light and warmth, a place where there was freedom to laugh, to celebrate life without eyes that watched and condemned.

The piper was leading the children to the base of the mountain, to the opening of the mine, and Leisel wondered why. But she was so entranced by his music that she didn't question him.

Until she saw that the mountain was trembling.

And the piper was leading the children directly inside.

"No!" she screamed as she tried to run to the front of the line. But her legs were heavy, weighted down with that terrible leaden feeling of a tormented dreamer. "Stop!"

He didn't stop. Heedless of her cries, he continued into the mine, and the children followed. One by one they disappeared into the dark mouth of the tunnel. Monika, Hans, Sigmund—Leisel watched as the children she loved were swallowed by the quaking mountain, as the man she loved led them into what must be certain death. And just as she had been helpless the night her mother had died, she could do nothing to stop this tragedy.

Stones were already raining down from the mountainside as the last child passed inside. Leisel stood outside the entrance, fighting a war within her own heart. Something was pulling her toward the mountain, beckoning her to follow him as the children had, but the mountain was going to cave in. Its collapse was becoming more obvious with every passing moment, with every boulder that came tumbling down the rocky crags.

"Leisel, come quickly."

She turned and saw him standing just inside the entrance, his hand stretched out to her.

"It's going to fall!" she shouted. "Summon the children and come out of there before there's a cave-in!"

He simply smiled and shook his head. "Come with me, Leisel. Please. Take my hand."

Although her heart told her to go to him, her eyes saw only the Grim Reaper. "You'll die—all of you!"

"Trust me, Leisel. Please . . . trust me."

She awoke with a start.

The gray morning, the trembling mountain, the horrible sound of falling rocks were all suddenly gone. It was still night, dark and silent, and she was still lying warm inside the circle of the piper's arms.

"What is it, my love?" he said, hugging her close.

She shivered and hid her face against his chest. "A dream," she said. "A terrible dream."

"Tell me about it."

It took her several moments to gather her thoughts and words. "You were in it, and me and the village children."

"Yes?"

"And it was all so awful. We were about to die."

"And . . ."

"And you were asking me to trust you. To follow you into the mines."

She felt his heartbeat quicken as his arms tightened around her. "And did you trust me, Leisel?" he asked. "Did you follow me?"

"I don't know," she said. "I woke before I gave you my answer."

"I see." He sounded disappointed, and she wished that she had said something different.

"I'm sorry," she said.

He bent his head down to her and kissed her gently as he pulled his cloak more tightly around her. "Go back to sleep, my lady," he said. "The morning will be here too soon."

Snuggled warm in his arms, Leisel drifted into a restless sleep. Her dreams were haunted by strange and contradictory images—visions of a man with moonlight in his hair, whose pipe gave forth a song sweet enough to make the heart weep or sing . . . and fiery sermons that warned her to beware of the devil, who deceived the foolish by disguising himself as an angel of light.

Ten

WHEN LEISEL WOKE the next morning, the piper wasn't lying beside her. He was standing at the edge of the meadow, staring into the forest. With one hand resting against a birch and his head slightly bowed, he seemed tired. The expression on his face was pensive and sad.

Leisel was surprised to see this vibrant man downcast, and she felt guilty when she remembered how disappointed he had been to hear the end of her dream.

The sun was already high in the sky, reminding her that she should return to the Schmidts. They would be expecting their breakfast soon, and she had to be there to prepare it. But she couldn't bring herself to leave him yet.

Slowly she stood and walked over to his campfire, where she knelt and began to stir the embers.

At the sound of her putting more wood on the fire he turned and, after a moment's hesitation, joined her. "Good morning, my lady," he said, sitting down beside her. "Did you sleep well?"

"Yes, thank you. And you, sir?"

His eyes trailed over her face and down to the bodice, which had become partially unlaced during the night. "I spent a pleasant night." Noting the darkness under his eyes, Leisel surmised that he hadn't slept at all.

"May I prepare a breakfast for you?" She grabbed a nearby branch and stirred the fire she had resurrected. "I would gladly make you—"

"No." He reached out and touched her where her tunic had fallen and bared her shoulder. "Leisel, who did this to you?" he asked as his fingertips brushed the garment away from her shoulder and upper back.

She realized that he was looking at her scars, and she blushed scarlet. Those scars were her shame, her constant and permanent reminder. "It doesn't matter," she said, yanking the blouse into place.

"It does." He pulled it back down and touched the puckered crisscrosses. "I want to know."

She said nothing as she bit her lower lip, trying to think of some pretty lie. But none came to mind. This man could see all the way through her. There was no point in lying to him.

"How much do you want to know?" she asked.

"I want to know it all."

"It happened here," she said, pointing to the stone pillar, "years ago when I was a child. The town council convicted my mother of witchcraft, brought her here, and burned her to death."

He heard the pain in her voice, and yet there was a certain sense of detachment, as though she had removed herself from a time and place too horrible to remember. "Did you see it happen?" he asked.

"Yes. They forced me to watch. They wanted to make sure I would remember. As though I could forget."

She walked up the pile of stones and he followed her. When she reached out to touch the smoke-blackened stake, he saw that her hand was trembling.

"She died rather quickly—" Leisel closed her eyes for a moment and swallowed "—because they had beaten her before. And because her hand was severed; she had lost a lot of blood."

He fought down the rage that was building inside him. The time for vengeance would come, but for now she needed his comfort and support. Reaching out, he placed his hand on her shoulder.

"Monika's mother didn't die so quickly," she said. "They killed her several years after my mother. First they accused her of causing Father Beck's cow to go dry. Then the baker's wife gave birth to a dead child and they said that Monika's mother had cursed it.

"Then the cooper swore that he saw her flying through the night on a stave that was dripping with blood. So they burned her, too. She had a cat, a beautiful black cat. It was her constant companion. They said it was a demon in animal form and that she . . . she committed unnatural acts with it. When they killed her, they tied the cat around her neck and burned it with her."

"Is that when they killed all the cats in the village?"

She nodded.

"And then the rats multiplied," he said. "Such things are happening all over. In my neighboring country they did the same thing. And the rats brought the plague that eventually spread to my land."

"So who is to say who is committing the evil?" Leisel said thoughtfully. "If people are dying because of these 'pious' acts, perhaps they aren't ordered by God, after all."

He slipped his hand beneath her glistening hair and ran his palm over the back of her tunic. "Tell me about the scars."

She shrugged, and once again he saw the detachment in her eyes. "After my mother was executed, they said they had to drive the devil from me. So every night for two weeks Father Beck and the baron stripped my clothes from me, tied me to the stake where they had killed my mother, and whipped me with the baron's riding crop. And every night Monika's mother waited in the trees to untie me and minister to my wounds. On the last night they caught her in the act of helping me. I think that was part of the reason they killed her later."

He couldn't listen anymore. If he heard her tell of one more savage act, he would lose the little control he'd maintained. "Let's leave this place," he said as he offered her his hand, then led her down the pile of stones.

When they reached the forest path, she turned and looked back at the stake. "They should have whipped me harder," she said bitterly, "or longer. They didn't drive the devil from me completely. I still want to see them dead. And I want to be the one to kill them, especially the baron."

The icy determination in her green eyes when she spoke those words chilled him. She was a strong woman, this lady of his. She had a power in her that could bring anything she desired into being. If she wanted the baron dead, he would die.

Or she would.

The fear that she would lose her battle kept him from sleeping. This was a battle to the death, and he wanted to make certain that it was the baron who died, not the woman he loved. Yet it was her war, and he had to let her fight it.

"Be careful. Remember that if you use the power inside you to bring harm to another, the greatest injury will be to your own spirit," he said, hoping his voice would reveal the depth of his concern for her, hoping it would make a difference.

She reached up and untwined the red silk scarf from her hair. "My mother gave me this," she said. "Whenever I touch it, I feel her presence, see?"

She placed it in his hand and he closed his palm around it.

"I feel only you," he said. "I feel your courage, your strength."

"Then keep it with you," she said. "And when you touch it, think of me." She turned, and before he could speak, she had disappeared into the forest.

He had intended to thank her, realizing that she had just given him her most prized possession. He had also wanted to tell her that he didn't need a talisman to think of her. Thoughts of her filled his every waking moment, just as the fear that he might lose her haunted his nights.

Leisel saw the two men standing in the road ahead, blocking her path. Even from a distance she recognized them as Rolf Gunter and Klaus Niklaus. Deep inside, Leisel knew that something was wrong. They were waiting for her.

For a moment she was tempted to turn and run back into the forest. But she thought of the children and knew that she couldn't afford the luxury of escape.

"Leisel," Gunter said when she reached them. "Your master, the baron, has been looking for you all morning. When you failed to prepare his breakfast, he checked the barn and realized that you had been gone all night."

"Father Beck believes you passed the night in the forest in the devil's embrace," Niklaus said, a suggestive lift to his eyebrows. Leisel thought of the day he had testified against her mother, proclaiming that he had witnessed her flight on a bloodstained pole. Considering the miller's love of ale, it was little wonder that he saw women flying beneath the light of the full moon as he stumbled drunkenly from the inn to his cottage on the edge of town. "The baron and Father Beck have asked us to escort you to the rectory," he said with exaggerated politeness.

She looked from one man to the other, searching their faces for any trace of compassion, but saw none. These were two of the faces that she had seen reflected in the red firelight that night years ago, contorted with hatred and evil.

Any attempt to appeal to their compassionate natures would prove fruitless.

So she lifted her chin and said, "I don't need an escort, thank you. I can surely find my way to the rectory alone. But if you wish to follow, you may."

"High-and-mighty, isn't she?" said Gunter as they fell into step behind her.

"Well, she won't be when the good Father finishes with her," replied Niklaus. "I always knew she was a witch, even when she was just a little one—with that white stripe in her hair. Heaven knows, no one else I've ever seen had such a mark as that. It's the devil's brand, for certain."

Leisel heard the rattle of Gunter's sword behind her as he said, "We can rest easy about one thing—if she's the devil's whore, Father Beck will prove it, and we'll have one less witch among us."

"We're going to have to search every inch of your body, Leisel," the priest said, "to see if the devil has put his mark upon you."

Revulsion swept over Leisel at the thought of these two men touching her. She looked across the rectory's bedchamber at the baron and hated him for the eager leer that split his pudgy face.

"Have you been out all night consorting with the devil?" Schmidt sneered. "Off indulging your carnal lusts while your master's house goes untended?"

In a gesture of defiance Leisel jerked the tunic off her shoulder and showed them the scars they had inflicted on her years before. "You don't have to search my body to find the devil's marks. They're right here. There are more marks than you can count all over my back and shoulders. Isn't that enough for you?"

The priest stepped up to her and slapped her hard across the face with the back of his hand. His long, yellow fingernails left red scratches across her cheek. "That will be enough, young woman. Disrobe immediately or we'll be forced to do it for you."

One by one Leisel shed her garments, dropping each article of clothing onto the stone floor. She could feel the men's eyes on her, hungry eyes that devoured her flesh as it was uncovered.

She recalled those nights so many years ago when these two men had made her strip and then beaten her. For the glory of God? She didn't think so. They did it to feed their own evil appetites.

Her rage gave her strength when the priest ordered her to lie across his bed. The baron brought a candle and held it over her naked body as they examined her breasts. Their hands were cold and damp as they moved over her, prodding and kneading. The hot wax dripped from the candle onto her skin, but she refused to flinch.

She closed her eyes tightly and tried not to think, not to feel, but it was impossible. She tried to imagine what she would do to them if she could, how she would kill them. But no death seemed painful enough to satisfy the fury that was building in her minute by minute as their hands moved lower and lower.

"There. There it is!" the priest exclaimed, touching the inside of her left thigh. "It's the devil's mark without a doubt. That's where the witch suckles the demon when she allows him to have carnal knowledge of her."

Leisel opened her eyes and looked down to see what he was referring to. It was nothing more than a tiny mole.

"For that you would accuse me of consorting with the devil?" she asked. "You both have marks such as that on your face. Are we to assume that you suckle a demon on your nose, Baron Schmidt?"

Once again she felt the sting of the priest's slap, this time across her right thigh. "You'll keep a civil tongue when you speak to us, girl," he said. "We'll listen to no such blasphemous remarks from one such as yourself. Get up and put your clothes on."

Then he turned to the baron. "We have our evidence now. If we can only find one witness, we'll be able to bring this devil's whore to justice."

As Leisel finished cleaning the kitchen that night after the evening meal, she tried to keep her anxiety under control. They had no witness, no one to swear that they had actually seen her performing an act of witchcraft. And they wouldn't find a witness. She had never performed a conscious act of witchcraft—except burning the baron's footprint, and no one had seen her do that.

She shuddered every time she thought of their cold, damp hands on her body. Damn them both to hell. No man had ever touched her that way. Her body was her own, the only thing in the world that was truly her own, and she had chosen to keep it to herself until she offered it to the man she loved.

For some reason she thought of the piper and felt a rush of shame. Would he think her soiled if he knew that she had been touched by their greedy, lecherous hands? Would he still call her his lady? What lady had ever been forced to suffer such indignities?

As she swept the floor she realized that for the first time the room was free of any signs of rat infestation. The rodents were gone, every last one of them. But the mine was still scheduled to open in three days. The town crier had made the announcement that evening. More than anything, she wanted to keep Monika and the rest of the children out of that mine. But for the moment she had a more pressing problem: how to keep herself alive. She could feel that circle of hate closing around her, tighter and tighter, dark and suffocating, squeezing the life out of her.

Her chores finished, she decided to go to the stable. In that solitary place, with only the soft lowing sounds of the animals and the scent of hay surrounding her, she could think and perhaps find a solution to her problems.

Tucking the broom into the corner, she left the kitchen. As she passed by the door to the dining hall, she heard a voice that made her stop. She melted into the shadows and listened.

"Trudl, she's your personal servant. You know her better than anyone in the world," she heard the baron saying. "Surely you've heard or seen something of her evil. An act of sorcery that we could use against her."

"No, Papa, I don't know anything."

The sound of a hand hitting flesh echoed through the house, and Leisel cringed, sensing her friend's pain.

"You've seen something. I know you have. And you'll tell me now or I'll—"

Trudl's scream of anguish cut Leisel deeply; she had to intervene. Trudl was still too weak to endure this kind of abuse. Storming into the room, Leisel was just in time to see Trudl cowering before her father, whose beefy fist was raised over her head.

"Stop!" Leisel said. "That will be enough. Take your hands off her!" Leisel's words shocked even her. She had never spoken to the baron in that way. Indeed, to her knowledge, no one had.

Stunned by her sudden outburst, he released Trudl. She edged away from him, then fled the room, sobbing into the apron that she held over her face. Recovering from his surprise, the baron caught Leisel by the shoulders and yanked her toward him. "Don't you ever interfere when I'm disciplining my family. Try that again, and I swear I'll kill you."

"You're going to kill me, anyway," Leisel heard herself saying. "You won't rest till you do."

His hands tightened around her shoulders until his stubby

fingertips bit into her flesh. "That's true," he said. "I'll see you burn, just like your mother. I look at you and I see her—her eyes, her hair." His gaze roamed over her breasts, and once again she saw that sickening light flickering in his eyes.

"Why did you hate her so?" she demanded. Even if it further endangered her life, she had to know the truth. "What did she ever do to you that you wanted to see her dead?"

He pulled her closer until her breasts were against his chest. "I loved your mother," he said, his voice slurred from too much ale. "The ungrateful bitch. I offered to marry her, a lowly peasant with a questionable reputation. But she spurned me. Me, a nobleman. The wealthiest man in Lower Saxony."

"So you killed her. You bore false witness against her and caused her to be burned at the stake just because she refused you."

"I didn't lie about her. She *was* a witch. She cast a spell on me. She made me want her. And, by God, I had her. I had her once before she died. And I'll have you, too." His meaning became all too clear as his hands began to roam all over her body. He pressed her back against the table, his bulky weight crushing her.

"No!" She gasped, trying to slap his hands away, but he tore her tunic open and rammed his thick fingers between her breasts. He began rubbing his body against hers, and she felt his hardness, which told her his intentions.

She screamed, knowing it would do no good. Even if Trudl or Eva heard her, no one would come to help her.

When he began to grapple with his codpiece, a coldness went through her. She would die before she would let him touch her. So it didn't matter what she said or did—even if he killed her—as long as he stopped.

"If you touch me, I'll tell Father Beck," she said, "and the entire council."

"He won't believe you. And even if he did, he wouldn't

care. You're a whore of the devil. Do you think he cares what I do to you?"

"Probably not. But I'll tell him what you did to your own daughter. How does the Church stand on the sin of incest?"

With a surge of satisfaction she watched him blanch. The punishment for incest was death. She knew that, and so did he. Some sins were forbidden, even to a baron.

"Don't you threaten me, girl," he said, throwing her backward against the table. The edge cut into her lower back as he twisted her hands behind her in a grip that made her fingers go numb and her wrists ache. "I'll show you what happens to a woman who threatens me."

Releasing her left hand, he ripped away his codpiece. Leisel looked down, dreading what she would see. But his threats were mightier than his manhood. The baron's sword lacked the steel necessary for assault.

"Witch!" he screamed, his humiliation complete. "No one but a witch could do that to me!"

He raised his hand and slapped her hard across the face. Pain shot through her head, stunning her into temporary submission. In a heartbeat she recovered and struck out with her free hand, curling her fingers into predatory talons. She clawed at his eyes, but he turned his head and her nails scraped long, scarlet welts across his cheek and down the side of his neck.

Crying out in pain, he released her and clasped both hands to his face. With all her might, Leisel shoved against his chest. Caught off-balance, he stumbled backward several paces, grunting in surprise and pain.

For a moment their eyes met and Leisel saw that he was shocked at the change in her, at her defiance of his authority. The baron wasn't accustomed to having his victims resist. She also saw his fury, his deep shame at his impotence and his burning malice toward her for having witnessed his disgrace.

"You're going to die, witch!" he muttered as he slid his hand beneath his tunic. "I'll send you to hell myself."

In a flash of awareness and horror, Leisel realized that he was reaching for the knife that he kept in a sheath at his side. She thought of her mother's severed hand and a coldness went through her, an icy determination. He wasn't going to mutilate her or kill her. Not if she could stop him.

Her physical strength had proved no match for him, but as she watched him pull the knife from its scabbard, time seemed to slow. Her panic fled, leaving her mind clear, her spirit strangely calm.

There was a formidable force deep inside her. She had always felt it, but never so intensely. Gathering that power into a weapon that was more destructive than the whetted blade of a sword, she hurled it toward the baron's shriveled manhood. Her head reeled as she summoned this dark stream of energy—the opposite of the healing power she had used to cure Trudl's headaches.

Herr Schmidt screamed as he fell to his knees on the floor, clutching his groin.

For a moment Leisel couldn't believe what she was seeing; it had worked! Her enemy knelt before her, groaning in agony that she had inflicted without even touching him. The power inside her was real, after all, and it could be used to heal or destroy. She was astonished, but she felt strangely empty.

Still trembling from exertion, Leisel pulled her torn clothes around her and fled. She ran out of the house seeking the darkness and peace of the night, the baron's cries still echoing in her ears and heart.

Eleven

NO MATTER HOW much she washed, the waters of the creek couldn't rinse away the soiled feeling. Their hands had touched her, cold groping hands that had made her feel as black as a smith's apron.

Standing here in the center of the creek that ran through the deepest part of the forest, Leisel knew that she was safe. Her enemies couldn't find her, here in her wooded sanctuary. But after having her body, mind, and spirit violated, she didn't feel safe—not even in the forest—and she didn't think she would ever feel safe again.

Besides, her rational mind reminded her, she couldn't stay here in the forest forever. But if she returned to the village, she would die. After what had happened tonight, the baron wouldn't rest until she was dead. She had witnessed his disgrace. As far as he was concerned, she had caused it. No. He couldn't allow her, a reminder of his shame, to live.

Sitting on a stone in the center of the creek, the water rushing around her chest and midriff, she scrubbed her breasts with her palms, but she could still feel the priest's probing, the baron's painful squeezing. She shuddered and fought back the urge to cry. If she started now, she might never be able to stop, and she needed to be strong right now.

If she allowed herself a moment of weakness, she was afraid that she might fall apart.

From behind her she heard a sound and whirled around, expecting to see a mob of angry villagers or at least one enraged baron. But it was the piper who stood at the edge of the creek. He gazed down at her, the moonlight shining silver on his hair.

With a rush of anxiety and embarrassment she crossed her arms over her bare breasts and slipped lower into the water.

But he smiled, his eyes soft and compassionate. Her fear began to ease. "Don't be afraid, my lady," he said, his voice more soothing than the cool water. "I've come to help, not hurt."

He stepped into the creek and waded toward her, the water not quite topping his thigh-high boots. When he reached her, he placed his hands on her shoulders in a gentle, nonthreatening touch and looked into her eyes. The concern she saw there made her wonder if he somehow knew what had happened to her.

She felt the tears well up from her throat and choke her. Emotions and thoughts she had been shoving to the back of her mind rushed forward, and there was nothing she could do to stop them.

"They touched me," she whispered. "They made me take off my clothes and lie on the bed while they touched me. They said they were looking for the devil's mark."

She saw him wince, as though he were feeling her shame, her pain. "I'm sorry, my lady," he said. With one hand he smoothed her damp hair. "I'm so sorry."

"I didn't feel like your lady," she said, the sobs thick in her throat. "I didn't feel like a person, just a thing."

He said nothing but leaned down and placed a kiss on her forehead.

"And then the baron tried to . . . to . . . but he couldn't . . ."

The humiliation, the fear, and the pain of the day came crashing in on her, overwhelming her. She couldn't hold back the tears any longer. "He was taking out his knife," she said, "and he was going to kill me, or at least hurt me, as he had my mother. But I didn't let him. I used the power inside me to hurt him first. It felt wrong, but I did it, anyway."

"How could it have been wrong," he said, stroking her hair, "if you're here before me now, alive and whole? Would it have been better if you were dead or injured? Where would have been the good in that?"

"I don't know. I'm so confused. And I feel so dirty. I don't think I'll ever be able to wash away their touch."

"Perhaps you can't," he said. "But I can."

With cupped palms he scooped up handfuls of the cool water and allowed it to trickle down her body, from her shoulders, over her breasts, and down her belly. Then, with hands that were gentle and comforting, he smoothed the glistening beads of water over her skin. His touch was light, his eyes kind and loving as he caressed her. There was no lust on his face when he looked into her eyes, and the only desire she saw was the sincere desire to heal.

"It's gone," he said as he continued the bath. "Their touch is gone. You'll never feel their hands on you again. From now on the only man who will ever touch you will be me."

Leisel closed her eyes, submitting to his ministrations. His hands were strong and warm and soothing, so different from the baron's or the priest's. Those vicious men had taken from her. This man was giving. They had harmed. He was healing those wounds. They hated her. And judging from the look in this man's eyes, he loved her deeply. She couldn't guess why, but she didn't care, as long as she could feel his love forever.

"Come," he said as he led her by the hand to the bank. "You need to be warm and rest. You've suffered a great deal today, and you need to regain your strength."

After drying her body with her tunic he draped his cloak around her. The garment was huge and heavy, enveloping her in its fullness. She buried her face in its soft folds and breathed in the subtle scent of his body.

With one arm around her waist he led her into the trees, to a spot where he had spread his bedroll. Like a tired child, she allowed him to ease her down onto the pallet, where she lay wrapped in his cloak.

He pulled off his wet boots, stretched out beside her, and pulled her against his chest. Her hands trailed over the soft fabric of the cloak, feeling the varying textures of its patchwork. Her fingers paused on a familiar square of silkiness.

"My scarf," she said, looking down at the red patch that was sewn over the left front. "You sewed my scarf into your cloak."

He smiled. "So I did."

She looked down at the many squares that made up the strange garment. "Are these all from women?" she asked, unable to hide the note of jealousy in her voice.

He threw back his head and laughed. The sound blended with the music of the creek and made her feel happy in spite of her jealousy. "Some of them, perhaps," he said. "But not all. They're bits of cloth that represent people and places all over the world who have meant something to me. I like carrying the reminders of my life with me wherever I go."

"And did you love those other women?" she asked, her lower lip protruding slightly.

He cupped her quivering chin in his palm and caressed her cheek. "Some of them, but I sewed your scarf over my heart. And it will be there forever."

She looked up into his eyes and saw that she was indeed special to him.

"I have a great fondness for you, my lady," he said as his fingertips trailed along her hairline, over her widow's peak and temple. "Could it be that you feel the same for me?"

Unable to trust herself to speak, she merely nodded.

He smiled. "I thought as much." Sitting up, he reached for his haversack at her side and pulled something from inside it. "When you gave me the scarf, I wanted to give you something in return. I realized that the scarf was the most precious thing you owned. I wanted my gift to be worthy of your sacrifice."

He pulled her up to sit beside him and placed the small gold crown in her lap. "You gave me that which you loved most. I offer you the same . . . my kingdom. I want you to be my queen, Leisel."

At first she could not answer. Moving gingerly, her fingers lifted the crown and turned it so that the gold and the pearls sparkled in the moonlight. "I can't be a queen," she said. "I'm just a peasant and—"

"You're the woman I want, the woman my country needs. I want to take you away from here, to a wonderful place where you won't have to live in fear, where you'll be treated with the respect you deserve."

Could it be true? A land without hate? A place where she could enjoy the sun on her face today, knowing that she would be alive to enjoy it tomorrow?

How she longed to go away with him at this moment. To escape. To be free of the weight that continually bore down on her. She wanted more than anything to say yes. But her fantasy proved fleeting when she thought of the baron, and Trudl, Monika, and the other pauper children.

"I want to," she said. "Believe me, I do. But I can't. I have things I must finish first." Reluctantly she placed the crown back in his hand.

"Be careful, Leisel," he said, his voice heavy with sadness and concern as he returned the crown to his bundle. With a sigh he gathered her into his arms and kissed her forehead. Then he lay down and pulled her against his side. "I've searched many years and many lands for you," he said as his arms tightened around her. "I couldn't bear to lose you now."

Werner Schmidt was furious, and the quantity of ale he had consumed during the evening hours hadn't improved his mood. He sat before the fire in his kitchen, a pile of gnawed bones on the floor at his feet, his pewter cup empty in his fist. He had eaten and drunk until his ample belly was distended and miserably stretched, but he could still feel the sting of humiliation—not to mention a deep burning in his groin, residue from that witch's devilish attack.

Women. He hated them. Always had. Ever since he could remember, they had laughed at him, shamed him because of his fatness, made him feel like less than a man. Other men he could bully with his wealth and authority. Other men couldn't see his impotence. But women . . . there was no hiding his shame from them.

Especially two of them. The witch and that ugly weasel of a child he had fed and clothed all these years, only to be betrayed by her. How dare she tell a mere servant what had passed between them! How dare she risk his life by revealing that which should have remained secret! If Trudl had told Leisel, who else had she told? Was it only a matter of time until everyone knew? Until he was brought before his own council and accused of the heinous crime of incest?

How could those men on the council know what it had been like for him all these years, married to a cold, spineless woman like Eva, who was plagued with headaches every time he came near her? How could they know that sometimes a man needed to touch and be touched by someone who didn't laugh at his body, at his occasional impotence? Besides, Trudl had enjoyed his lovemaking, even if she had pretended not to, even if she had cried and begged him to leave her alone. She had said those things only because she had thought it was expected of her, but the council wouldn't

understand. If she told anyone, he would lose everything
. . . maybe even his life.

The baron stood and wiped his mouth on his sleeve.
There was only one thing to do: make sure that Trudl didn't
tell anyone else.

He looked down on her as she slept, and for a moment he
felt a twinge of tenderness for this girl who was his only
child. But the feeling passed quickly when he thought of
how she had betrayed him. He had told her again and again
how important it was that she not reveal their little secret to
anyone. God knows, he had warned her if she let anyone
know what they had done together, he would kill her.

She woke and looked up at him with those lashless, brown
eyes. She was so ugly. He wondered how he could have ever
brought himself to touch her. He had been lonely. And he
had needed to feel like a man with someone, even a child.
He hated the fear and revulsion in her eyes when she looked
up at him. He wanted to wipe that look away, so that he
would never have to see it again.

"Father, no." She was going to plead again. Dear God,
how he hated to hear her pleading. "Please don't."

"That's not why I'm here, Trudl," he said, noticing how
she crossed her arms over her breasts to shield herself from
him. As though she hadn't welcomed his caresses. What a
hypocrite she was. What a filthy, lying little hypocrite!

"What do you want?"

He could hear her fear, smell it. It made him feel stronger
somehow. He could feel the tightness in his groin, a heavi-
ness that he hadn't felt in a while. He felt like a man again.

"You told Leisel about us," he said. "After I warned you
not to. After I told you that I'd kill you if you did."

"No . . . Father, I didn't tell her, but—"

His hands closed over her throat. He was surprised how
small it was, how delicate. It was going to be so easy.

She deserved to die.

He had given her life. And it was his to take away.

He squeezed and watched as her brown eyes widened, then bulged. Her thin body thrashed beneath him, fighting for life, but it was no contest because he was so much heavier.

It was all so easy.

He threw her body over the edge of the ravine and watched as it rolled down the cliff toward the river. There. No one would find her. At least not for days or weeks, and by then he would find a way to blame her death on Leisel.

Of course, by then the witch would be dead, too. The next time he saw her, he would do the same thing to her. If one killing had been simple, what was one more?

He would think of a way to tie their deaths together. The villagers were stupid. They would believe any story he told them. For now Trudl would be missing, and he would be the distraught father. By the time she was found, he would have thought of a story.

He turned to leave and his heart nearly stopped. Standing behind him, silhouetted in the moonlight, was the witch. His groin contracted with pain at the very sight of her, and he instinctively covered his manhood with his hands.

Although he had just sworn to kill her the next time he saw her, he couldn't bring himself to move toward her. His body remembered all too well the pain she had inflicted with her demon's power. She might not be an easy kill, after all . . . not like Trudl. Werner Schmidt stood there, gripping his codpiece, trembling in his kidskin slippers, not knowing what to do. But before he could decide, the decision was made for him.

Before his astonished eyes, she disappeared. She simply faded into the night air and was gone.

Schmidt couldn't move, he couldn't breathe, and he couldn't believe what he had just seen. Then he saw a shadow gliding through the trees to his right, but it wasn't the shape of a woman. It was the form of a giant wolf.

Twelve

"HE KILLED HER! He murdered Trudl!" Leisel sprang up from the pallet, clutching the piper's cloak around her.

When he noticed that she was shivering violently, he sat up and hugged her to him. "What do you mean? What is it, my love?"

Her eyes hot with tears, she buried her face in her hands. "The baron, he killed Trudl. I saw him in a dream. He was throwing her body over a cliff. It's happened, I tell you. I know it."

His eyes searched her face for a long moment, then he sighed. "It seems there's no sin too great for that man to commit. I've seen a lot of evil in my years, but none so dark as that. What kind of man kills his own child?"

Leisel swallowed her tears as a look of cold determination came over her face. "He has to be stopped. It's already too late for Trudl. Soon it'll be too late for Monika and the other children."

He reached for the short sword that lay on the pallet by his side. As he lifted it, the stag's head crest sparkled, the rubies and emeralds glittering in the moonlight. "I'll stop him," he said. "I've known all along it would come to that. I was only waiting for the right time."

She reached out and put her hand on the sword, lowering it to the ground. "He's my enemy, not yours. I'll do it."

"It would be better for me to kill him than for you to do so. I would kill him for justice, not revenge. You hate him, I don't. If you spill his blood out of hate, you've allowed him to corrupt you as well."

Her pretty face hardened, losing all of its youthful softness. "Hate, justice, or revenge . . . it's all the same to me, as long as Werner Schmidt dies. And he'll die by my hand."

She rose, dropped his cloak to the ground, and dressed quickly. Turning back to him, she said, "This is mine to do. If you love me, you'll leave it to me."

He watched as she walked away. The urge to stop her was strong, but he let her go. It was one of the most difficult things he had ever done in his life. She was strong, but her hatred and desire for vengeance had weakened her. And what concerned him most was that she didn't know how vulnerable she was.

He reached into his haversack and drew out the pack of cards. Shuffling, he chose one and held it up to the moonlight. It was the Strength card, a picture of a beautiful young woman holding a lion's head in her grasp, taming the beast. He sat and stared at the card, absorbing its wisdom and message: true strength could only be found when one balanced passion with logic.

She had asked him not to intervene and he wouldn't. At least not now. If she wouldn't allow him to lift his sword in her defense, he would help the only way he could. He closed his eyes and sent her the strength depicted on the ancient card that he held in his hand. He only hoped it would be enough.

Leisel sat on the gnarled log, her head bent over her mother's journal. After a lengthy search she had found what she was looking for, and she was reading the passage very carefully. The passage on shape changing. She couldn't believe what she was reading . . . that it would really work.

But lately she had been listening to her heart, and her heart told her it would.

Werner Schmidt was quite the worried father—or at least his fellow townsmen thought so. Everyone in the village had been searching for Trudl for three days. Apparently beside himself with grief, Schmidt led the search, wringing his hands, threatening one moment, pleading the next.

This morning the searchers had fanned out into the forest, having combed every byway and barn in the village and neighboring farms. Many of the villagers had given up and gone back to their daily work, wishing the good baron and his wife Godspeed in finding their lost child.

Leaving the others behind, Schmidt had gone deeper into the forest, with his crossbow and a quiver of arrows for protection. The villagers praised his bravery but refused to follow him. Everyone knew that evil churned in the darkest part of the woods.

Schmidt found a small glade and a tree to lean against for an afternoon nap. The diligent search—climbing ladders in and out of barn lofts, rummaging through the brush—had worn him out, but the effort had been necessary. Any worried father would have done the same.

He was glad that he had disposed of her body far from town. If he had chosen a closer spot, they surely would have found her by now. He hadn't expected this kind of community dedication to finding a missing girl—especially a homely maiden like his daughter.

In the shade of the tree he soon drifted off into a deep, peaceful sleep, uninterrupted by disturbing dreams. But after only a few minutes he awoke with a start. At first he wasn't sure what had awakened him, then he saw it, a beautiful deer standing only a few feet from him.

Such an easy target was too great a temptation for the hunter in him to resist. Carefully he lifted his crossbow and pulled an arrow from the quiver on his back. With practiced skill he fitted the arrow to the bow and let it fly. Although he missed his target, the deer's side, the arrow plunged into her right flank. She struggled, trying to run, but fell after going only a few paces.

Schmidt laughed and ran over to her, pulling his knife from its sheath. In that moment he felt like a man, the hunter with its prey, the master with a helpless creature at his mercy. He intended to kill the deer slowly, inflicting as much pain as it could bear, but not enough to cause its death . . . until he tired of the game.

His smile widened as he dragged the sharp edge of his knife along the creature's back and watched her hide twitch and jerk. The frightened deer reminded him of the thrill he'd felt when he had once held a woman at knife point. He had felt like a man then, too. Besides, she was a witch. She had lifted her hand against him. "If thy hand offend thee, cut it off," Father Beck had said, and he had.

He wondered if he could cut the deer's hooves off, one by one, while it was still alive. Would it kick him? Or was it already weak enough to submit? As he reached for the animal's right front hoof he heard it . . . a low, rumbling growl behind him. He spun around and saw an enormous wolf standing not three feet from him, its teeth bared, its shackles standing on end.

It was black, as black as the deepest part of the forest on a moonless night, and it had a strange silver streak running down the right side of its head. Werner Schmidt looked into the wolf's eyes, and his heart thudded against his ribs.

Its eyes weren't those of an animal; they looked human. Only human eyes could be so filled with hate.

They were hungry eyes.

Baron Werner Schmidt knew, even as he gripped his

knife, that this wolf wasn't like the other one, the silver one. This wolf was stronger.

And he knew that he was about to die.

The piper heard the screams from the edge of the creek where he was filling his flask. With his hand on his sword hilt he plunged through the woods, heading toward the sound. He arrived just as the baron fell to the ground, his arms flailing over his face and throat in an attempt to shield himself from the wolf's teeth.

Drawing his sword, the piper waited and watched as the magnificent animal pinned its prey to the ground, its teeth bared, a low growl rumbling from its broad chest. The baron reached for his knife, but no sooner had he pulled it from its sheath than the wolf had his forearm in its teeth. Shrieking his fear and pain, the man dropped the knife and struck out at the wolf with his left hand.

The piper watched, fascinated by the animal's grace and agility as it mauled its victim. The beast bit his hands and arms and clawed at his chest. Although the baron left himself open, the wolf never went for the jugular to cause the man severe harm.

"You don't really want to do it," he whispered. "You could, but you don't choose to. You were given your power and knowledge to bring healing and life, not destruction and death."

The wolf raised its head. Their eyes met, and the animal seemed to hear and comprehend what he said. It hesitated for a long moment, looked down once more at Herr Schmidt, then turned and retreated into the woods. Following at its heels was another wolf, a silver one who limped; its right front foot was severed at the first joint.

The piper waited until both wolves had disappeared into the trees, then he walked over to the baron.

Picking himself up off the ground, Schmidt lifted his

knife and pointed it at the piper. "You did this!" he shouted, waving the blade under his nose. "Father Beck said you were a devil. You caused that wolf to attack me."

The piper smiled bitterly. "I probably just saved your life, you fool. But I didn't do it for you. I did it for the woman I love. If she had killed you, it would have poisoned her spirit, and I wanted to spare her that."

Schmidt sneered as he circled his opponent. "You think you saved me from that wolf?" He chuckled. "I would have cut its throat and had its heart for my soup pot if you hadn't come along when you did." He took a couple of practice stabs at the piper. "Maybe I should cut your heart out instead."

The piper sidestepped each thrust, his sword lifted in readiness. "Don't be stupid," he warned him. "I have a sword, you have a knife. Besides, you're no match for me."

"Oh, you think not? We shall see about that." The baron lunged again, and once more the piper effectively dodged his attack. "If you force my hand, I'll kill you," he said.

"You'll try. Let's see if you succeed."

With one deft blow the piper laid a thin, red line across the baron's belly, but still the man wouldn't halt his advance. In his fury Schmidt had lost all sense of judgment.

With three steps the baron closed the distance between them and stabbed at the piper's chest. The tip of the knife caught his biceps as he deflected the attack. Blood trickled warm and red down his arm.

The piper looked at his torn sleeve and watched as the red color stained the fabric. He thought of Leisel's mother tied to a stake as red flames roared around her, and her young daughter was forced to look on. He thought of the scars on Leisel's back and the deeper ones on her heart. He thought of the children who'd been doomed to toil in the dark mine, and of Trudl, lying lifeless at the bottom of a cliff.

Enough was enough. This man had caused too much pain for too many people.

The piper lifted his sword, thrust downward, drove the blade through the baron's heart . . . and ended the suffering.

Leisel stood before the honorable town council of Hamelin, her hands clenched into fists beneath her apron, her chin held high. She stared defiantly across the table at Father Beck, whose dark eyes burned in his gaunt face as he returned her hostility. She thought of the last time she had stood before them, only weeks before. She had been a child then. So many things had happened, so many crises that had forced her through this difficult rite of passage. She was a woman now.

The recent events would make little difference in the outcome for this village, she realized, but she had changed.

"You are accused of killing two citizens of Hamelin, Baron Werner Schmidt, and his daughter, Trudl," the priest said. "You slew the baron by use of your devil's magic, and you murdered Trudl Schmidt, a young woman in your keeping, with your bare hands and cast her body into a ravine."

From the front of the crowded room came a sob as Eva Schmidt collapsed into the arms of her friends. Leisel didn't turn around. She couldn't look upon the woman's pain right now. She had troubles enough of her own. Besides, Eva had just borne witness against her that might cause her death. Although Leisel knew that Eva had suffered a long and grueling interrogation at the hands of the council—Father Beck in particular—she still felt betrayed when the noblemen had finally wrested the condemning "evidence" from her mistress.

"I didn't harm Trudl Schmidt," she said, her voice clear and strong above the crowd's murmurings. "She was my friend."

The priest smiled bitterly. "But you *did* harm Trudl. Eva

Schmidt has testified here today that you practiced witchcraft on the girl and nearly brought about her death only a few days ago. Isn't that true?"

Leisel winced as Eva's treason stabbed even deeper. She had only been trying to help, and Eva knew that; yet under duress she had given this council the evidence they needed to convict her.

"Ask Eva Schmidt why I gave those herbs to her daughter," Leisel said. "Ask her if my medicine was given with evil intentions or in love."

"We have no proof of your intentions, only your actions. The baroness has sworn that you gave Trudl unsanctified herbs and that the potion nearly killed the girl. We can only assume that you knew what you were doing and meant to bring about her death. After the baroness rescued her child from your evil sorcery, you made yet another attempt and succeeded in killing the girl."

Leisel bit her lip, fighting back the urge to tell her side of the story. She could speak the truth, but it would make no difference; this council was determined to convict her, and they would. If she were to tell the council about Trudl's pregnancy and the baron's incest, she would be destroying Trudl's memory and Eva Schmidt's life. And all for naught, as they would condemn her no matter what she said.

"Then there's the matter of Baron Schmidt." The priest leaned back and scratched at the festering rash on his forearm. "The baron was found dead only this afternoon, his body badly mauled by a wolf."

"And how can that be my fault?" she asked.

"Don't make your situation any worse by trying to mislead this council. We aren't ignorant of the ways of witches, having dealt with several of them before. The tracks around the baron's body were made by a wolf that was much too large for any creature made by God. That animal was a demon, conjured by the devil . . . or by one of his servants."

"I conjured no demon," she said, her voice as steady as her gaze.

For a moment the priest was nonplussed, but he quickly recovered. "And the second set of tracks that were found near the body, the tracks of another giant wolf who was lame . . . we've dealt with that evil spirit before. It was laid to rest, as you will soon be."

"No spirit is laid to rest who was murdered unjustly," she said. "A soul such as that returns again and again, seeking vengeance on those who harmed her."

Leisel saw the fear in the priest's eyes, and it pleased her deeply. Her mother's memory and magic still had the power to terrify her enemies.

"And when the men of this village arrested you there in the meadow," he said, "they found you reading this." He pointed to her mother's book, which lay on the heavy oak table near his right hand. "Do you deny that this book is filled with the devil's potions and charms?"

"It's my mother's diary, a record of those she helped during her short life. The record should have been longer, but her life was ended almost before it began—"

"Your mother isn't on trial here!" he shouted. "You are! And you'd better remember that this council holds your life in its hands."

"It doesn't matter how I address this honorable council, does it, Father?" she said. "You intend to put me to death no matter what I say. You—not this council—*you* want to see me dead for a number of reasons. Mostly because you want my mother's book. You want to read it yourself and discover the power inside those pages, a power you recognize as being stronger than your own. My mother's journal is all you've ever really wanted, and you'll murder me to get it."

The crowd gasped. Father Beck jumped to his feet, his eyes blazing. He rushed around the table and grabbed Leisel by her hair, yanking her head back so that she was forced to look up at him. "You'll die because you're a *witch!*" he screamed. "You'll die because you've consorted with the devil himself. This council hereby condemns you to burn at the stake that your soul may be purged by the fires of hell!"

The passage was narrow, dark, and damp as the piper made his way carefully through the main tunnel of the mine. In places he had to get down on his hands and knees and squeeze his broad shoulders through tunnels that seemed too small for a badger, let alone a child. The jagged edges of rocks imbedded in the walls scraped his arms raw, and his lungs ached from breathing the foul vapors.

Shuddering, he thought of the hours, days, and years that the children had spent in this miserable hole. He thought of the baron and how he had felt watching the man die. He hadn't taken pleasure in it; he never took satisfaction in killing, but he had felt relief.

With Schmidt dead, the mine would be closed. But only for a short time. Having governed a nation, the man in the multicolored cloak knew that the town's greed would win in the end. The mine would be reopened and the children would be down in it again, breathing in the poisonous air, dying day by day, denied the warmth of the sun.

It mustn't happen. He had to stop it.

He walked on and on through the labyrinth, searching, knowing the solution was there somewhere, perhaps just around the next bend.

Finally, he turned a corner and saw it . . . a tiny beam of light just ahead. He had his answer. The mountain that had brought death to so many would provide the passageway through which he would lead the survivors to new lives.

He thought of Leisel, of her dreams of this ominous mountain. When the time came, would she find the courage to listen to the voice deep in her heart? Would she place her trust in him and follow him through the black shadow of death into the golden sunlight?

Half an hour later he exited the mine and stood watching the sun as it set behind Koppelberg Mountain. Night was on its way, a warm, summer night, but for some reason he felt chilled. There was something in the air, something that disturbed the tranquillity of the twilight hour.

He closed his eyes and listened to the voices that spoke only to the heart.

Fear gripped him as he felt the waves of hatred and violence that billowed toward him from the direction of the forest. He started to run, and his fear mounted with each step. He wished to be as fleet-footed as a deer that he might reach her more quickly. He had to get there in time.

He thought of the smoke-blackened stake, of the scars on her back. A surge of terror nearly overwhelmed him as he neared the site. It was *her* terror; he knew it.

His feet found the speed they needed.

Thirteen

THE COLOR RED swirled all around her. The color of anger, of hatred, of violence and fire. The villagers were gathering still more wood, as though the fire weren't hot enough already. Leisel felt the heat on her face, arms, and chest, making her skin crawl and quiver. She heard their maniacal laughter, and she remembered.

A hundred faces looked up at her, their eyes glittering red in the firelight. Hungry eyes.

At the edge of the circle stood Monika, in the very spot where Leisel herself had once stood. The priest held the child's head, forcing her to witness the execution. Leisel despised him for making her watch. She hated him for the words she heard him saying: "Look! Watch and see what happens to the devil's whore!"

The ring of flames leapt higher as her fellow townsmen piled on the wood. She heard someone scream. A woman. Then she realized it was her.

The smoke curled around her, thick and suffocating as it seared her lungs. Choking spasms tore through her. She twisted against the chains that held her hands above her head, knowing that even if she were free of them, she was too weak to climb through the wall of flames that leapt around her.

Then she heard it . . . a change in the voice of the crowd. The shouts of anger turned to cries of fear. She didn't see him until he burst through the flames, a giant stag, bigger than any deer could be. His coat glowed the color of golden sunlight, his rack of horns like fine, polished silver. She didn't believe what she was seeing, but the cries of the crowd told her that they saw him, too. As though in a dream, she felt him brush against her and in an instant the chains fell away from her hands and waist.

She smelled the acrid scent of scorching hair and clothes as the fire closed around them. Finding a strength she didn't know she had, she reach out and grasped the stag around his neck. A moment later she was on his back and they were bounding down from the pile of rocks. Three leaps and they were through the mob, headed into the forest.

Leisel closed her eyes, tightened her arms around his neck, and slipped into unconsciousness.

The priest sat in the middle of the clearing before a roaring campfire. By the light of the flames he read the ancient words, penned years before by the woman who had been his enemy, the woman he had destroyed. His head was bent as he studied his treasure, the sleeves of his monk's robe rolled up to the elbow. He was ready to work.

From a leather pouch that was tied to his waist sash he pulled some packets of powders, a couple of birch leaves, bits of oak bark, and two feathers from a raven's wing. Referring to the book in his lap, he carefully measured a pinch of powder and crumpled the leaves.

After binding all the ingredients into a thin black scarf, he held the cloth over the flames.

"Bring my enemy back to me," he whispered to whatever spirits might be listening. "She escaped a few hours ago. Bring her back."

He dropped the amulet into the fire and waited anxiously

to see what kind of magic would unfold around him. Nothing happened. Impatiently he stirred the flames with a piece of kindling, but the cloth refused to catch fire. Puzzled, he knelt before the fire and leaned over it, staring down into the flames. What strange enchantment was this? A kerchief that wouldn't burn?

Suddenly the blaze exploded in a shower of red and gold sparks, and in an instant the priest's hair and clothing were aflame. Screaming, he threw himself onto the grass and rolled, trying to extinguish the searing fire that engulfed him.

Moments later he lay on his back, staring up at the moon but seeing nothing as he wandered, lost, through the torment of his pain. He had put out the fire. But not before his body had been permanently scarred, forever crippled. Not before Father Beck had suffered the fires of hell he had warned his flock about for so many years.

The next morning when Leisel woke, she was lying on the ground. She didn't know where she was or what had happened to her. Slowly she sat up and looked around. Behind her was the forest, to her right flowed the River Weser, and beyond the river in the distance rose Koppelberg Mountain, cold and gray in the predawn light. At her feet and down a steep incline lay the town of Hamelin.

She tried to stand, but every movement caused her great pain. Her body's stiffness and her scorched, torn clothes brought the night's events crashing back into her memory.

She looked around for the stag who had been her strange rescuer, only to find herself alone. Not even the birds had awakened yet. Shivering, she unconsciously snuggled deeper into the heavy garment that had been wrapped around her shoulders. Taking notice, she saw that it was the piper's cloak. The sight of it warmed her and lessened the chill of the morning.

She wasn't sure exactly what had happened the night

before, how much of it was nightmare, reality, or illusion. But she knew that her life had been spared, and having come so close to death, Leisel realized more than ever how much she wanted to live.

As she looked down on the sleeping village she thought how benign it appeared. Who would guess that inside those quaint cottages with their thatched roofs slept the mob who had demanded her death? Farmers who tilled the soil. Craftsmen who created a village's necessities with their skillful hands. Families, men and women, who nurtured their children and made love to each other at night. Paupers and noblemen with one thing in common: Last night they had all wanted to see her burn alive.

As she watched, a heavy blanket of fog drifted down from the top of the mountain toward the village. The cold mist settled over the roofs of the cottages, lending an eerie, almost sinister, gray cast to the scene.

Leisel shivered again and clutched the cloak even tighter around her. The village would be stirring soon, and she would have to disappear into the forest—deep into the forest. Perhaps she could find the piper and tell him what had happened to her. Maybe he could help her escape to a safer place.

But no. She dismissed the thought the moment it entered her mind. How could she leave without the children? If she stayed, she would die. If she left, she would never forgive herself for deserting them.

A moment later she heard it—a light, clear note that floated through the fog. It was the music of the piper's flute, an enticing melody that she had never heard him play before. The tones were the highest, most delicate sounds she had ever heard. The song sounded like the laughter of children. She strained her ears to catch every note.

From the corner of her eye she caught a movement. The door to one of the cottages opened, and the cooper's daughter stepped into the street. One by one the other cottage doors began to open, and children of all sizes joined Kristen. From out of barns, from under shop steps, from the finest homes to the goatskin tents on the edge of the town, children poured into the streets. Like sleepwalkers, they turned and marched up the road toward the River Weser. With every step they gained momentum, and in a few moments they were dancing and skipping to the beat of the music.

Leisel turned toward the river, her eyes searching the bank. For a moment the fog parted, and she saw him standing there, his pipe to his lips, his foot tapping out the rhythm. In spite of her sadness, the sight of him made her smile, and she reached down to touch her scarf where he had sown it to the front of the cloak.

The children were a lively army as they quickly made their way up the road toward the river. Leisel thought of the rats, of how they had marched to their deaths. She saw Monika, Hans, and Sigmund among the dancers, and her heart froze.

No. Surely he wouldn't.

He had warned her against taking vengeance. He had cautioned her about acting out of hate. He couldn't. Not innocent children.

Forgetting her battered body, Leisel stood and ran down the hill. They were nearly to the riverbank by the time she reached the street. As she ran, she heard the men and women of Hamelin stirring from their sleep, waking to the realization that their children were trundling off down the road.

"Where are they? Where are the children?" they said as they stumbled into the street.

"Listen . . . it's the piper again. Hear his song?"

"They're following him. Look down the road."

"Where is he taking them?"

"To the river. God in heaven! He's going to drown them like he did the rats!"

Leisel heard them running behind her, but they were too

far away. She might be able to reach the piper and the children in time, but the villagers couldn't.

"No, look! He's not taking them to the river," said an excited voice behind her. "He's leading them to the mountain."

It was true. He was leading his marchers straight to Koppelberg Mountain . . . and into the mine.

As she ran, Leisel remembered her dream: the gray fog, the piper's song, the children following him into the tunnel.

Nearing the hill, she looked up and saw that the mountain was trembling, just as it had in her dream. Rocks, large and small, rained down the hillside. At the mine entrance the piper halted, still piping, as the children passed inside.

"No! Don't let them go in!" Leisel cried as she ran up to the base of the hill where he stood. "The mountain is falling. They'll die."

One by one they filed inside, and only after the last child had entered the mine did he stop playing. Stepping inside the entrance, he beckoned to her. "Come, Leisel. Hurry, my love!"

She stood just outside the mine, looking up at the pebbles that cascaded down around her. She heard the mountain groan and felt the earth tremble beneath her feet. Whirling around, she saw the villagers scrambling up the path behind her. Again they were the shouting, angry mob of the previous night, their faces contorted with rage.

Leisel turned back to the piper. His eyes beseeched her. "Come with me, my lady," he said. "Trust me, please."

Leisel remembered the death card . . . the Grim Reaper and the corpses that lay at his feet. She thought of the children inside that black cave. "But we'll die," she said. "We'll all be killed."

"Do you really believe I'd let you die, Leisel? Listen to your heart. What does it tell you?"

Leisel heard her mother's words: *Follow your heart, Leisel. It will never lead you astray.*

For a moment she stood still and listened. With the world crashing around her, she reached deep inside, found that quiet place, and heard the soft whispers of her spirit.

Following her heart's coaxing, Leisel took three steps toward the mine entrance, closed her eyes, and reached out to the piper. She felt his hand, warm and strong, close around hers as he pulled her inside and into his arms.

A moment later there was a deafening roar as the side of Koppelberg Mountain collapsed, sending a shower of stones and boulders careening over the mine entrance. From the path below, the villagers saw the hole that had just swallowed their children disappear beneath the avalanche.

Those parents in the crowd watched in silent agony, unable to comprehend what had happened. For long moments they waited for the rocks to stop falling.

When the deluge ceased, the dust settled, and the ground stopped shaking, there was no sign of the mine entrance.

No one spoke; they only stared . . . at the mountain . . . at each other.

Finally Helga spoke, expressing the villagers' thoughts. "They're dead. We didn't pay him for killing the rats. So he took our children. They're all dead."

Behind them, at the edge of the forest, a giant silver wolf stood, watching the entire scene. Satisfied, she turned and disappeared into the forest.

Afterword

SEVENTY-FIVE YEARS later the worst wave of the Black Plague swept the continent of Europe, including Lower Saxony and the village of Hamelin. Millions of people died, but a large region of the Bohemian Forest was spared. This area was inhabited by a tribe of strange people bearing Germanic surnames, who were said to have extraordinary mystical powers. These people claimed that their great-grandparents had come to this land as children. Their forefathers said they had traveled through a dark cavern, across fields and rivers to a castle in the mountains, led by a mysterious man who wore a multicolored cloak and played a silver flute, and by his lady, a young woman of exceptional beauty and courage.